Lessing, Doris
   The memoirs of a survivor.

| DATE DUE | | |
|---|---|---|
| Sept 12 | SEP 01 | JUN 1 0 1987 |
| Sept 16 | JUL 8 79 | MAR 1 8 |
| Oct. 8 | APR 2 3 1980 | |
| Oct 24 | JAN 1 2 1981 | |
| Jan 10 | MAR 2 8 1981 | |
| Jan. 22 | DEC 1 6 1981 | |
| MAY 2 4 1976 | AUG 1 0 1982 | |
| JUN 1 8 | NOV 1 5 1982 | |
| AUG 2 3 | JAN 2 8 1983 | |
| MAY 1 0 197 | MAY 2 1 1983 | |
| AUG 1 0 7 | MAY 1 3 1985 | |

# THE MEMOIRS
# OF A SURVIVOR

# THE MEMOIRS
# OF A SURVIVOR

Doris Lessing

ALFRED A. KNOPF · NEW YORK · 1975

THIS IS A BORZOI BOOK
PUBLISHED BY ALFRED A. KNOPF, INC.

Copyright © 1974 by The Octagon Press

All rights reserved under International and Pan-American Copyright
Conventions. Published in the United States by Alfred A. Knopf, Inc., New
York, and distributed by Random House, Inc., New York. Originally
published in Great Britain by The Octagon Press Ltd., London.

Library of Congress Cataloging in Publication Data
Lessing, Doris May, (date) The memoirs of a survivor.
I. Title.    PZ3.L56684Me3    [PR6023.E833]    823'.9'14   74-21294
ISBN 0-394-49633-7

Manufactured in the United States of America
Published June 2, 1975
Second Printing Before Publication

*This book is for my son Peter.*

# THE MEMOIRS
# OF A SURVIVOR

WE ALL remember that time. It was no different for me than for others. Yet we do tell each other over and over again the particularities of the events we shared, and the repetition, the listening, is as if we are saying, "It was like that for you, too? Then that confirms it, yes, it was so, it must have been, I wasn't imagining things." We match or dispute like people who have seen remarkable creatures on a journey: "Did you see that big blue fish? Oh, the one you saw was yellow!" But the sea we travelled over was the same, the protracted period of unease and tension before the end was the same for everybody, everywhere; in the smaller units of our cities—streets, a cluster of tall blocks of flats, a hotel—as in cities, nations, a continent. . . . Yes, I agree that this is pretty highflown imagery considering the nature of the events in question: bizarre fish, oceans, and so forth. But perhaps it wouldn't be out of place

here to comment on the way we—everyone—will look back
over a period in life, over a sequence of events, and find much
more there than they did at the time. This is true even of
events as dispiriting as the litter left on a common after a
public holiday. People will compare notes, as if wishing or
hoping for confirmation of something they had seemed to
exclude altogether. Happiness? That's a word I have taken up
from time to time in my life, looked at—but I never did find
that it held its shape. A meaning, then; a purpose? At any
rate, the past, looked back on in this frame of mind, seems
steeped in a substance that had seemed foreign to it, was ex-
traneous to the experiencing of it. Is it possible that this is the
stuff of real memory? Nostalgia—no, I'm not talking of that,
the craving, the regret—not that poisoned itch. Nor is it a
question of the importance each one of us tries to add to our
not very significant pasts: "*I* was there, you know. *I* saw that."

But it is because of this propensity of ours that perhaps
I may be permitted the fancy metaphors. I *did* see fish in that
sea, as if whales and dolphins had chosen to show themselves
coloured scarlet and green, but did not understand at the time
what it was I was seeing, and certainly did not know how
much of my own personal, experience was common, was
shared: this is what, looking back, we acknowledge first—
our similarities, not our differences.

One of the things we now know was true for everybody,
but which each of us privately thought was evidence of a
stubbornly preserved originality of mind, was that we ap-
prehended what was going on in ways that were not official.
Not respectable. Newscasts and newspapers and pronounce-
ments were what we were used to, what we by no means
despised: without them we would have become despondent,
anxious, for of course one must have the stamp of the official,

particularly in a time when nothing is going according to expectation. But the truth was every one of us became aware at some point it was not from official sources that we were getting the facts which were building up into a very different picture from the publicised one. Sequences of words were crystallising events into a picture, almost a story: *And then this happened, and so-and-so said* . . . but more and more often these were words dropped during a casual conversation, and perhaps even by oneself. Yes, of course! one would think. That's it. I've known that for some time. It's just that I haven't actually heard it put like that, I hadn't grasped it. . . .

Attitudes towards Authority, towards Them and They, were increasingly contradictory, and we all believed that we were living in a peculiarly anarchistic community. Of course not. Everywhere was the same. But perhaps it would be better to develop this later, stopping only to remark that the use of the word "it" is always a sign of crisis, of public anxiety. There is a gulf between "Why the hell do they have to be so incompetent!" and "God, things are awful!" just as "Things are awful" is a different matter again from "It is starting here, too," or "Have you heard any more about it?"

I shall begin this account at a time before we were talking about "it." We were still in the stage of generalised unease. Things weren't too good, they were even pretty bad. A great many things were bad, breaking down, giving up, or "giving cause for alarm," as the newscasts might put it. But "it," in the sense of something felt as an immediate threat which could not be averted, no.

I was living in a block of flats, which was one of several such blocks. I was on the ground floor, at earth-level; not, as it were, in some aerial village with invisible paths beaten from window to window by the inquisitive or the speculative eye

among birds following their roads, while traffic and human
affairs were far below. No, I was one of those who looked up,
imagining how things might be up there in the higher regions,
where windows admitted a finer air and where front doors led
to the public lifts and so down, down, to the sound of traffic,
the smells of chemicals and of plant life . . . the street. These
were not flats built by a town council, the walls scribbled with
graffiti, the lifts stained with urine, the walls of lobbies smeared
with excrement: these were not the vertical streets of the poor,
but were built by private money, and were heavy, were settled
widely over the valuable soil—the formerly valuable soil. The
walls were thick, for families who could afford to pay for
privacy. At the entrance was a largeish hall, carpeted, and
there were even stands of flowers, artificial but handsome
enough. There was a caretaker. These blocks were models of
what such buildings should be for solidity and decency.

But by that time, with so many people gone from the
city, the families who lived in these blocks were not all the
class for whom the buildings had been put up. Just as, for
years, all through the eroding streets of the poor, empty
houses had been taken over by squatters, settling in families
or groups of families—so that for a long time it had been
impossible to say, "This is a working-class area, this is homo-
geneous"—so, too, in these great buildings once tenanted only
by the well-to-do, by the professional and business people,
were now families or clans of poor people. What it amounted
to was that a flat, a house, belonged to the people who had
the enterprise to move into it. So, in the corridors and halls of
the building I lived in, you could meet, as in a street or a
market, every sort of person.

A professor and his wife and his daughter lived in the
twin set of rooms to mine down the corridor; immediately

above me was a family of Indians with many relatives and dependants. I mention these two sets of people because they were closest to me, and because I want to make the point that it is not as if an awareness of what went on behind walls and ceilings had been lacking before the start of—what? Here I do find difficulty, because there is nothing I can pinpoint, make definite. . . . Now I am talking not about the public pressures and events we encapsulate in words like "They," "Them," "It," and so on, but my own private discoveries which became so urgent and which were making such a claim on me at that time. I can't say, "On such and such a day I knew that behind the wall a certain quality of life was being lived." Not even, "It was in the spring of that year that . . ." No, the consciousness of that other life, developing there so close to me, hidden from me, was a slow thing, coming precisely into the category of understanding we describe in the word "realise," with its connotation of a gradual opening into comprehension. Such an opening, a growing, may be an affair of weeks, months, years. And of course one can "know" something, and not "know" it. (One can also know something and then forget it!) Looking back, I can say definitely that the growth of that other life or form of being behind that wall had been at the back of my mind for a long time before I *realised* what it was I had been listening to, listening for. But I can't set down a date or a time. Certainly this inner preoccupation predated the other, public concern to which I've given—I hope it is not thought frivolously—the word "it."

Even at my dimmest and thickest, I did know that what I was becoming conscious of, what I was on the edge of *realising,* was different in quality from what in fact went on around me: above my head, the lively, busy, warming family life of the Indians, who came, I believe, from Kenya; and different

again from what I heard from the rooms inhabited by Professor White and his family—the wall of whose kitchen was also
the wall of mine, through which, although it was a thick wall,
we had news of each other.

My not realising, or allowing myself to take in, the full implications of the fact that something was going on behind the
wall of my living-room was because beyond it was a corridor.
To be precise about it, what I was hearing was impossible. The
sounds that come from a corridor, even a much-used one, are
limited. It is for getting from one place to another: people
walk along corridors singly, in pairs, in groups, talking or not
talking. This corridor led from the front hall of the building,
past the door into my flat, then on to the Whites' front door,
and so around to the flats on the east side of the ground floor
of the building. Along that corridor went the Professor and
the members of his family and their visitors, myself and my
visitors, the two families from the east side and their visitors.
So it was used a good deal. Often one had to be aware of feet
and voices, distanced by the solidity of that wall, but I would
say to myself, "That must be the Professor—surely he is early
today?" Or, "That sounds like Janet back from school."

Yet there did come that moment when I had to admit
that there was a room behind that wall, perhaps more than
one, even a set of rooms, occupying the same space as—or,
rather, overlapping with—the corridor. The realisation of what
I was hearing, the knowledge that I had been aware of something of the kind for a long time, became strong in me at the
time that I knew I would almost certainly have to leave this
city. Of course, by now everyone had a sense of this: knowing
that we would have to leave was not confined to me. This is an
example of something I have already mentioned: an idea coming into everyone's mind at the same time and without inter-
vention from the authorities. That is to say, it was not an-

nounced through the loudspeakers, or on public platforms, in the newspapers, on the radio, the television. God knows that announcements of all kinds were continually being made; yet these were not absorbed by the populace as was this other information. On the whole, people tended to disregard what the authorities said—no, that is not quite true. The public information was discussed and argued and complained about, but it had a different impact. Suppose I said it was regarded almost as an entertainment? No, that is not right either. People did not act on what they heard, that is the point—not unless they were forced to. But this other information, coming from no one knew where, the news that was "in the air," put everyone into action. For instance, weeks before the official announcement that a certain basic foodstuff was to be rationed, I ran into Mr. Mehta and his wife in the hall—the old couple, the grandparents. They were dragging between them a sack of potatoes; I, too, had a supply. We nodded and smiled, mutually commending our foresight. Similarly I remember Mrs. White and myself exchanging good mornings on the paved area in front of the main entrance. She said, quite casually, "We shouldn't leave things too long." And I replied, "We've got some months yet, but we ought to be making preparations, I agree." We were talking about what everyone was, the need to leave this city. There had been no public intimation that people should leave. Nor, for that matter, was there ever any recognition on the part of the authorities that the city was emptying. It might be mentioned in passing, as a symptom of something else, as a temporary phenomenon, but not as the big fact in our lives.

There was no single reason for people leaving. We knew that all public services had stopped to the south and to the east, and that this state of affairs was spreading our way. We knew that everyone had left those parts of the country except for bands of people, mostly youngsters, who lived on what they could find: crops left ungathered in the fields, animals that had escaped slaughter before everything had broken down. These bands, or gangs, had not, to begin with, been particularly violent or harmful to the few people who had refused to leave. They even "co-operated with the forces of law and order," as the newscasts put it. Then, as food became more scarce, and whatever the danger was that had first set populations on the move away from it came closer, the gangs became dangerous, and when they passed through the suburbs of our city, people ran inside and stayed out of their way.

This had been going on for months. Warnings, first by rumour, then through the news sources, that gangs were moving through such-and-such an area, where the inhabitants had gone behind their locked doors until the danger had passed; that new gangs were approaching this or that area, where people would be well-advised to look after their lives, and their property; that another district, formerly dangerous, was now safe again—such alarms were part of our lives.

Where I lived, on the north side of the city, the streets were not used as roadways for the migrating gangs until a long time after the southern suburbs had become accustomed to them. Even when parts of our own town took anarchy for granted, we in the north talked and thought of ourselves as immune. The trouble would vanish, dissolve, take itself off. . . . Such is the strength of what we are used to, the first two or three appearances of gangs in our northern suburbs seemed to us isolated incidents, not likely to be repeated. Slowly we came to understand that it was our periods of peace, of normality, and not the days of looting and fighting, which were going to be unusual now.

And so—we would have to move. Yes, we would go. Not quite yet. But it would soon be necessary, and we knew it . . .

and all this time my ordinary life was the foreground, the lit area—if I can put it like that—of a mystery that was taking place, had been going on for a long time, "somewhere else." I was feeling more and more that my ordinary daytime life was irrelevant. Unimportant. That wall had become to me— but how can I put it? I was going to say, an obsession. That word implies that I am ready to betray the wall, what it stood for—am prepared to resign it to the regions of the pathological? Or that I felt uneasy then or now about my interest in it? No, I was feeling as if the centre of gravity of my life had moved, balances had shifted somewhere, and I was beginning to believe—uncomfortably, still—that what went on behind the wall might be every bit as important as my ordinary life in that neat and comfortable, if shabby, flat. I would stand in my living-room—the colours were predominantly cream, yellow, white, or at least enough of these to make it seem that walking into the room was walking into sunlight—I would wait there, and look quietly at the wall. Solid. Ordinary. A wall without a door or a window in it: the door from the lobby of the flat was in the room's side wall. There was a fireplace, not in the middle of it but rather to one side, so that there was a large expanse of this wall quite empty: I had not put up pictures or hangings. The "white" of the walls had darkened and did not give off much light unless the sunlight lay on it. Once there had been wallpaper. It had been painted over, but under the paint outlines of flowers, leaves, birds were still visible. When in the mornings sun did fall on part of that wall, the half-obliterated pattern showed so clearly that the mind followed suggestions of trees and a garden into a belief that the wash of light was making colour—greens, yellow, a certain shade of clear shell pink. It was not a high wall: the ceilings of the room were a comfortable height.

As you can see, there is nothing I can think of to say about

this wall that could lift it out of the commonplace. Yet, standing there and looking at it, or thinking about it while I did
other things about the flat, the sense and feel of it always in
my mind, was like holding to one's ear an egg that is due to
hatch. The warm smooth shape of one's palm is throbbing.
Behind the fragile lime, which, although it can be crushed
between two fingers, is inviolable because of the necessities of
the chick's time—the precise and accurate time it needs to get
itself out of the dark prison—it is as if a weight redistributes
itself, as when a child shifts position in the womb. There is the
faintest jar. Another. The chick, head under its wing, is pecking its way out, and already the minutest fragments of lime
are collecting on the shell where in a moment the first black
starry hole will appear. I even found I was putting my ear to
the wall, as one would to a fertile egg, listening, waiting. Not
for the sounds of Mrs. White's, or the Professor's, movements.
They might have just gone out or just come in; the ordinary
sounds of the corridor might in fact be there. No, what I was
hearing was from somewhere else. Yet they were ordinary
sounds in themselves: furniture being shifted; voices, but from
very far off; a child crying. Nothing clear. But they were
familiar; I had been hearing them all my life.

One morning I stood with my after-breakfast cigarette—I
allowed myself this one real cigarette a day—and through
clouds of blue coiling smoke looked at how the yellowness of
the sun stretched in a foreshortened oblong, making the wall
itself seem higher in the middle than at its ends. I looked at
the glow and the pulse of the yellow, looked as if I were
listening, thinking how, as the seasons changed, so did the
shape and extent and position of this patch of morning light—
and then I was through the wall and I knew what was there.
I did not, that first time, achieve much more than that there

were a set of rooms. The rooms were disused, had been for
some time. Years, perhaps. There was no furniture. Paint had
flaked off the wall in places, and lay in tiny shards on the
floorboards with scraps of paper and dead flies and dust. I did
not go in, but stood there on the margin between the two
worlds, my familiar flat and these rooms which had been
quietly waiting there all this time. I stood and looked, feeding
with my eyes. I felt the most vivid expectancy, a longing: this
place held what I needed, knew was there, had been waiting
for—oh, yes, all my life, all my life. I knew this place, recognised it, and before I had actually absorbed the information
through my eyes that the walls were much higher than mine,
that there were many windows and doors, and that it was a
large, light, airy, delightful flat, or house. In a farther room I
glimpsed a painter's ladder; and then, just as the sunlight faded
out on my wall when a cloud absorbed the sun, I saw someone
in white painter's overalls lifting a roller to lay white paint
over the faded and stained surface.

I forgot this occurrence. I went on with the little routines of
my life, conscious of the life behind the wall, but not remembering my visit there. It was not until a few days later that I
again stood, cigarette in hand in the mid-morning hour, looking through drifting smoke at the sunlight laid there on the
wall, and I thought, Hello! I've been through there; of course
I have. How did I manage to forget? And again the wall dissolved and I was through. There were more rooms than I had
suspected the first time. I had a strong sense of that, though I
did not see them all. Nor did I, on that occasion, see the man
or the woman in overalls. The rooms were empty. To make
them habitable, what work needed to be done! Yes, I could see
that it would take weeks, months. . . . I stood there marking
fallen plaster, the corner of a ceiling stained with damp, dirty,

or damaged walls. Yet it was on that morning when I was beginning to understand how much work needed to be done that
I saw, just for the ghost of a second—well, what? But I can
hardly say. Perhaps it was more of a feeling than something
seen. There was a sweetness, certainly—a welcome, a reassurance. Perhaps I did see a face, or the shadow of one. The
face I saw clearly later was familiar to me, but it is possible
that that face, seen as everything ended, appears in my memory
in this place, this early second visit: it had reflected itself back,
needing no more to use as a host or as a mirror than the emotion of sweet longing, which hunger was its proper air. This
was the rightful inhabitant of the rooms behind the wall. I had
no doubt of it then or later. The *exiled* inhabitant; for surely
she could not live, never could have lived, in that chill empty
shell full of dirty and stale air?

When I again knew myself to be standing in my living-
room, the cigarette half burned down, I was left with the con-
viction of a promise, which did not leave me, no matter how
difficult things became later, both in my own life and in these
hidden rooms.


□   □   □


The child was left with me in this way. I was in the
kitchen, and, hearing a sound, went into the living-room, and
saw a man and a half-grown girl standing there. I did not
know either of them, and advanced with the intention of
clearing up a mistake. The thought in my mind was that I
must have left my front door open. They turned to face me.
I remember how I was even then, and at once, struck by the

bright, hard, nervous smile on the girl's face. The man—
middle-aged, ordinarily dressed, quite unremarkable in every
way—said, "This is the child." He was already on the way out.
He had laid his hand on her shoulder, had smiled and nodded
to her, was turning away.

I said, "But surely . . ."

"No, there's no mistake. She's your responsibility."

He was at the door.

"But wait a minute. . . ."

"She is Emily Cartright. Look after her." And he had gone.

We stood there, the child and I, looking at each other.
I remember the room had a wash of sun: it was still morning.
I was wondering how the two had got in, but this already
seemed irrelevant, since the man had gone. I now ran to the
window: a street with a few trees along the pavement; a bus-
stop with its familiar queue of people waiting; and on the
wide pavement opposite, underneath the trees there, some
children from the Mehtas' flat upstairs playing with a ball—
dark-skinned boys and girls, all dazzling white shirts, crisp
pink and blue dresses, white teeth, gleaming hair. But the man
I was looking for—not a sign.

I turned back to the child; but now I took my time over
it, and was wondering what to say, how to present myself, how
to handle her—all the pathetic little techniques and tricks of
our self-definition. She was watching me, carefully, closely:
the thought came into my mind that this was the expert as-
sessment of possibilities by a prisoner observing a new jailer.
Already my heart was heavy: anxiety! My intelligence was not
yet making much of what was happening.

"Emily?" I said tentatively, hoping that she would choose
to answer the questions in my mind.

"Emily Mary Cartright," she said, in a manner that matched

her bright impervious voice and smile. Pert? At any rate a
hard, an enamelled presence. I was trying to get past or around
it; I was conscious that I was desperately making signals—my
smile, gestures—which might perhaps reach something softer
and warmer that must be there behind that cold defence of
hers.

"Well, will you sit down? Or can I make you something to
eat? Some tea? I do have some real tea, but of course . . ."

"I'd like to see my room, please," she said. And now her
eyes were, quite without her knowing it, an appeal. She needed,
she needed very much, to know what walls, what shelter she
was going to be able to pull around her, like a blanket, for
comfort.

"Well," I said, "I haven't thought yet . . . I don't quite . . .
I must . . ." Her face seemed to shrivel. But she preserved her
bright desperation. "You see," I went on, "I wasn't expecting
. . . Let's see, now." She waited. Stubbornly, she waited. She
knew that she was to live with me. She knew that her shelter,
her four walls, her den, the little space that was hers and which
she could creep into, was here somewhere. "There's the spare
room," I said. "I call it that. But it isn't very . . ." But I went,
and I remember how helplessly and unhappily I did, into the
little front lobby, and through it to the spare room.

The flat was on the front of the building, the south side.
The living-room took up most of the space: its size was why
I had taken the flat. At the end away from the entrance lobby,
so that you had to walk through the living-room to get to it,
was the kitchen, on the corner of the building. This was quite
large, with cupboards and storage space, and was used for
eating as well. From the entrance lobby went two doors, one
to the living-room, one to the room I called a spare room. This
room was connected with the bathroom. My bedroom was on

the front of the building, reached from the living-room. The bathroom, lobby, spare room took up the same space as my bedroom, which was not large. It will be seen that the spare room was very small. It had a small high window. It was stuffy. There was no way of making it attractive. I never used it except for keeping things in or, with apologies, for a friend staying the night.

"I'm sorry that it is so small and dark. . . . Perhaps we should . . ."

"No, no, I don't mind," she said, in the cool jaunty way which was so much hers; but she was looking at the bed with longing, and I knew she had found her refuge, hers; here it was at last. "It's lovely," she said. "Oh, yes, you don't believe me—you don't know what . . ." But she left the possibility of an explanation of what she had been experiencing, and waited, her whole body expressing how she wanted me to leave.

"And we'll have to share the bathroom," I said.

"Oh, I'll be ever so tidy," she assured me. "I'm really very good, you know, I won't make a mess, I never do."

I knew that if I were not in this flat, if she did not feel she must behave well, she would be between the blankets, she would already be far away from the world.

"I won't be a tick," she assured me. "I must get tidy. I'll be as quick as I can."

I left her and waited for her in the living-room, first standing by the window looking out, wondering perhaps if fresh surprises were on the way. Then I sat down—rather, I imagine, in the attitude of *The Thinker,* or some such concentrated pose.

Yes, it was extraordinary. Yes, it was all impossible. But, after all, I had accepted the "impossible." I lived with it. I had abandoned all expectations of the ordinary for my inner world,

my real life in that place. And as for the public, the outer
world, it had been a long time since that offered the normal.
Could one perhaps describe that period as "the ordinariness of
the extraordinary"? Well, the reader should have no difficulty
here: these words are a description of the times we have lived
through. (A description of all life?—probably, but it is not
much help to think so.)

But these words convey perfectly the atmosphere of what
was happening when Emily was brought to me. While everything, all forms of social organization, broke up, we lived on,
adjusting our lives as if nothing fundamental was happening.
It was amazing how determined, how stubborn, how self-
renewing were the attempts to lead an ordinary life. When
nothing, or very little, was left of what we had been used to,
had taken for granted even ten years before, we went on talking
and behaving as if those old forms were still ours. And indeed,
order of the old kind—food, amenities, even luxuries—*did*
exist at higher levels; we all knew that, though of course those
who enjoyed these things did not draw attention to themselves. Order could also exist in pockets, of space, of time—
through periods of weeks and months or in a particular district. Inside them, people would live and talk and even think
as if nothing had changed. When something really bad happened, as when an area got devastated, people might move out
for days, or weeks, to stay with relatives or friends, and then
move back, perhaps to a looted house, to take up their jobs,
their housekeeping—their order. We can get used to anything
at all; this is a commonplace, of course, but perhaps you have
to live through such a time to see how horribly true it is. There
is nothing that people won't try to accommodate into "ordinary
life." It was precisely this which gave that time its peculiar
flavour; the combination of the bizarre, the hectic, the frighten-

ing, the threatening—an atmosphere of siege or war—with what was customary, ordinary, even decent.

For instance, on the newscasts and in the papers they would pursue for days the story of a single kidnapped child, taken from its pram perhaps by some poor unhappy woman. The police would be combing the suburbs and the countryside in hundreds, looking for the child, and for the woman, to punish her. But the next news flash would be about the mass deaths of hundreds, thousands, or even millions of people. We still believed, wanted to believe, that the first—the concern about the single child, the need to punish the individual criminal, even if it took days and weeks and hundreds of our hard-worked police force to do it—was what really represented us; the second, about the catastrophe, was, as such items of news had always been for people not actually in the threatened area, an unfortunate and minor—or at least not crucial—accident, which interrupted the even flow, the development, of civilisation.

This is the sort of thing we accepted as normal. Yet for all of us there were moments when *the game we were all agreeing to play* simply could not stand up to events: we would be gripped by feelings of unreality, like nausea. Perhaps this feeling, that the ground was dissolving under our feet, was the real enemy . . . or we believed it to be so. Perhaps our tacit agreement that nothing *much*—or at least nothing irrecoverable—was happening was because for us the enemy was Reality, was to allow ourselves to know what was happening. Perhaps our pretences, everyone's pretences, which in the moments when we felt naked, defenceless, seemed like playacting and absurd, should be regarded as admirable? Or perhaps they were necessary, like the games of children who can make playacting a way of keeping reality a long way from their weaknesses?

But increasingly, all the time, one had to defeat the need simply to laugh: oh, not a good laughter—far from it. Rather, bellows and yells of derision.

For instance again: in the same week that a horde of two hundred or so hooligans had surged through our neighbour-hood—leaving a corpse on the pavement across the street from my windows, leaving smashed windows, looted shops, the re-mains of bonfires—a group of middle-aged women, self-ap-pointed vigilantes, were making formal protests to the police about an amateur-theatricals group some youngsters had set up. This group had written and put on a play describing the tensions within an ordinary family living in a block of flats like ours, a family which had taken in half a dozen refugees from the eastern counties. (As long as travellers were with the migrating gangs, they were "hooligans," but when they hived off to find shelter with some family or household, they were "refugees.") A household that had held five people suddenly held twelve, and the resulting frictions led to adultery and an incident where "a young girl seduced a man old enough to be her grandfather," as the good women indignantly described it. They managed to organise a not very well-attended meeting about the "decay of family life," about "immorality," about "sexual indulgence." This was comic, of course. Unless it was sad. Unless—as I've suggested—it was admirable; a sign of the vitality of the said "ordinary life" which would in the end defeat chaos, disorder, the malevolence of events.

Or what can one say about the innumerable citizens' groups that came into existence right up to the end, for any ethical or social purpose you could think of: to improve old-age pensions, at a time when money was giving way to barter; to supply vitamin tablets to school children; to provide a visit-ing service for housebound invalids; to arrange formal legal adoption for abandoned children; to forbid the news of any violent or "unpleasant" event, so as not to "put ideas into young people's heads"; to reason with the gangs of hooligans as they came through the streets, or alternatively to birch them; to go around and about the streets, exhorting people to "restore a sense of decency to their sexual practices"; to agree not to eat the meat of cats and dogs; and so on, and on, and on— there was really no end to it. Farce. Spitting into a hurricane; standing in front of a mirror to touch up one's face or straighten a tie as the house crashes around one; extending the relaxed accommodating hand of the Royal handshake to a barbarian who will certainly bend and take a good bite out of it—such similes come to mind. Such analogies were being made then, of course, in the conversations that were our meat and drink, and by the professional comedians.

In such an atmosphere, in a time of such happenings, that an unknown man should arrive in my home with a child, saying she was my responsibility, and then leave without further remark was not as strange as all that.

When Emily at last came out of her bedroom, having changed her dress and washed from her face what looked like an assault of miserable tears, she said, "The room will be a bit small for Hugo and me, but it doesn't matter a bit."

I saw that she had beside her a dog—no, a cat. What was it? An animal, at any rate. It was the size of a bulldog, and shaped more like a dog than a cat, but its face was that of a cat.

It was yellow. Its hide was harsh and rough. It had a cat's eyes and whiskers. It had a long whip-like tail. An ugly beast. Hugo. She sat herself down carefully in my deep old sofa opposite the fireplace, and the beast got up beside her and sat there, as close as he could get, and she put her arm about him. She looked at me from beside the animal's cat face. They both looked at me, Hugo with his green eyes, and Emily with her defensive shrewd hazel eyes.

She was a large child, of about twelve. Not a child, really; but in that halfway place where soon she would be a girl. She would be pretty, at least good-looking. Well-made: she had small hands and feet, and good limbs that were brown with health and sun. Her hair was dark and straight, parted on one side, held with a clip.

We talked. Or, rather, we offered each other little remarks, both waiting for that switch to be turned somewhere which would make our being together easier. While she sat there silent, her brooding dark gaze, her mouth with its definite possibilities of humour, her air of patient thoughtful attention made her seem someone I could like very much. But then, just as I was sure she was about to respond in kind to my attempts, my feeling of pleasure in her potentialities, there would come to life in her the vivacious self-presenting little *madam*—the old-fashioned word was right for her: there was something old-fashioned in her image of herself. Or perhaps it was someone else's idea of her?

She chattered: "I'm awfully hungry, and so is Hugo. Poor Hugo. He hasn't eaten today. And neither have I, if the truth must be told."

I made my apologies and hastened out to the shops to buy whatever cat or dog foods I could find for Hugo. It took some time to find a shop which still stocked such things. I was an object of interest to the shop assistant, an animal-lover, who applauded my intention to stand up for my right to keep "pets" in these days. I also interested one or two of the other customers, and I was careful not to say where I lived, when one asked me, and went home by a misleading route, and made sure I was not being followed. On the way I visited several other shops, looking for things I usually did not bother with, they were so hard to track down, so expensive. But at last I did find some biscuits and sweets of a quite decent quality— whatever I thought might appeal to a child. I had plenty of dried apples and pears, and stocks of basic foodstuffs. When at last I got back home, she was asleep on the sofa, and Hugo was asleep beside her. His yellow face was on her shoulder, her arm was around his neck. On the floor beside her was her little suitcase, as flimsy as a small child's weekend case. It had in it some neatly folded dresses and a jersey and a pair of jeans. These seemed to be all she owned in the way of clothes. I would not have been surprised to see a teddy or a doll. Instead there was a Bible, a book of photographs of animals, some science-fiction paperbacks.

I made as welcoming a meal as I could for both her and Hugo. I woke them with difficulty: they were in the exhausted state that follows relief after long tension. When they had eaten, they wanted to go off to bed, though it was still mid-afternoon.

And that was how Emily was left with me.

In those first few days, she slept and she slept. Because of this, and because of her invincible obedience, I was unconsciously thinking of her as younger than she was. I sat waiting quietly in my living-room, knowing that she was asleep, exactly as one does with a small child. I did a little mending for her, washed and ironed her clothes. But mostly I sat and looked at that wall and waited. I could not help thinking that to have a child with me, just as the wall was beginning to open itself up, would be a nuisance, and in fact she and her animal were very much in the way. This made me feel guilty. All kinds of emotions I had not felt for a long time came to life in me again, and I longed simply to walk through the wall and

never come back. But this would be irresponsible; it would
mean turning my back on my responsibilities.

It was a day or two after Emily came: I was beyond the
wall, and I kept opening doors or turning the corners of long
passages to find another room or suite of rooms. Empty. That
is, I did not see anyone, although the feeling of someone's
presence was so strong I even kept turning my head quickly,
as if this person could be expected to step out from behind a
wall in the few seconds my back had been turned. Empty but
inhabited. Empty but furnished . . . Wandering there, between
tall white walls, from room to room, I saw that the place was
filled with furniture. I knew these sofas, these chairs. But why?
From what time in my life did they date? They were not my
taste. Yet it seemed that they had been mine, or an intimate
friend's.

The drawing-room had pale pink silk curtains, a grey
carpet with delicate pink and green flowers laid on it, many
small tables and cabinets. The sofas and chairs were covered
in tapestry, had pastel cushions placed exactly here and there.
It was a room too formal and too self-sufficient ever to have
been mine. Yet I knew everything in it. I walked there, slowly
filling with irritated despair. Everything I looked at would
have to be replaced or mended or cleaned, for nothing was
whole or fresh. Each chair would have to be re-covered, for the
material was frayed. The sofas were grimy. The curtains had
little rents and the roughened patches moths leave, each with
its minuscule holes. The carpet showed its threads. And so with
all the many rooms of this place, which was giving me a feeling
of things slipping away from me through clumsy and stiff
fingers. The whole place should be cleared out, I kept saying
to myself. It should be emptied, and what was in it now
should be burned or thrown away. Bare rooms would be better

than this infinitely genteel shabbiness, the gimcrackery. Room after room after room—there was no end to them, or to the work I had to do. Now I kept looking for the empty room that had in it a painter's ladder and a half-glimpsed figure in overalls: if I could see this, it would mean a start had been made. But there were no empty rooms, every one was crammed with objects, all needing attention.

It must not be thought that all my energy was going into this hidden place. For days at a time I did not think of it. The knowledge of its being there, in whatever shape it was using for the moment, came to me in flashes during my ordinary life more and more often. But I would forget it, too, for days. When I was actually through that wall, nothing else seemed real; and even the new and serious preoccupations of my life —Emily and her attendant animal—slid away, were far off, were part of another distant life which did not much concern me. And this is my difficulty in describing that time: looking back now, it is as if two ways of life, two lives, two worlds, lay side by side and closely connected. But then, one life excluded the other, and I did not expect the two worlds ever to link up. I had not thought at all of their being able to do so, and I would have said this was not possible. Particularly now, when Emily was there; particularly when I had so many problems that centred on her being with me.

The main problem was, and remained for some time, that she was so infinitely obliging and obedient. When I got up in the morning, she was already up, dressed in one of her neat little dresses, the clothes of a good child whose mother needs her children to be well-dressed, even remarkably so. Her hair was brushed. Her teeth were cleaned. She was waiting for me in the living-room, with her Hugo, and instantly she began chattering, offering this or that to me, how she had slept

marvellously, or how she had dreamed, or how she had had
this amusing or foolish or valuable thought—and all in a rushing, almost frantic way of forestalling some demand or criticism from me. And then she began about breakfast, how she
would "adore" to cook it—oh, she would simply love to,
please, for really she was ever so handy and capable. And so
she and I would go into the kitchen, the beast padding behind
us, and Hugo and I sat watching her preparations. And she
was, indeed, competent and nifty. And then we ate whatever
it was, Hugo's head at her waist-level, his eyes calmly watching
her, me, our hands, our faces, and when he was offered a bit of
food he took it delicately, like a cat. Then she would offer to
wash up. "No, no, I love washing-up, incredible as it might
seem, but I really do!" And she washed up and made the
kitchen neat. Her bedroom had been tidied already, but not
her bed, which was always a nest or womb of coiled blankets
and pillows. I never reproved her for this; on the contrary,
I was delighted that there was one place she felt was her own,
that she could make her refuge, where she could hide away
from this really awful need always to be so bright and good.
Sometimes, unpredictably, during the day, she went to her
room—abruptly, as if *something* had been too much. She
shut the door and, I knew, crawled into the heap of disorder,
and there she lay and recovered—but from what? In the living-
room she sat on my old sofa, her legs curled up, in a pose
which was as much an offering to what might be expected of
her as was her manner, her obedience. She watched me, as if
anticipating commands or needs, or she might read. Her taste
in reading was adult: seeing her there, with what she had
chosen, made her bright child's manner even more impossible,
almost as if she were deliberately insulting me. Or she would
sit with her arm around the yellow beast, and he licked her

hand, and put his cat's face on her arm and purred, a sound which rumbled through the rooms of my flat.

Had she been some kind of a prisoner?

I did not ask. I never asked her this question. And she did not volunteer information. Meanwhile my heart ached for her, recognising her manner for what it was; and at the same time, while I was really quite soft and ridiculous with pity for her, I was in a frenzy of irritation because of my inability ever, even for a moment, to get behind the guard she had set up. There she was, the solemn, serious little girl, in her good little girl's dress, showing every mark of the solitary child, all self-consciousness and observation, and then off she'd go, chattering and rattling, being "amusing," offering me little skills and capacities as a return for—but what? I did not feel myself to be so formidable. I almost felt myself not to exist, in my own right. I was a continuation, for her, of parents, or a parent, a guardian, foster-parents. And when we left here, presumably I would hand her over to someone else? The man who had given her into my care would come to take her back? Her parents would arrive? Otherwise, what was I going to do with her? When I started my travels north or west, joining the general movement of the population away from the southern and eastern parts of the country, what would I be moving into? What sort of life? I did not know. But I had not envisaged a child, never a responsibility of such a total sort . . . and besides, even in the few days she had been here, she had changed. Her breasts were shaping, pushing out the child's bodice. Her round face with its attractive dark eyes needed very little to shape it into a young girl's face. A "little girl" was one thing, and bad enough—"child with her pet"—but the "young girl" would be quite another, and particularly in these times.

It will sound contradictory when I say that another thing

that bothered me was her indolence. Of course there wasn't
very much to do in my flat. She sat for hours at my window
and watched, absorbed in everything that went on. She entertained me with comment: this was a deliberate and measured
offering; she had been known, it was clear, for her "amusing"
comments. Here again I did not know quite what it was I had
to reckon with, for these were certainly not a little girl's perceptions. Or perhaps I was out-of-date, and this was what one
had to expect in this time, for what strains and stresses did
children now not have to accept and make part of themselves?

Professor White would come out of the lobby and down
the steps, and then stop, looking up and down the street, almost
in a military way: *Who goes there!* Then, reassured, he stood
for a moment: almost he could be imagined pulling on a pair
of gloves, adjusting a hat. He was a slight man, young for a
professor, still in his thirties; a precise, an ashy, man, with
everything in his life in its proper place. On to Emily's face
would come a smile as she watched him, a sour little smile, as
if she was thinking, I've got *you,* you can't escape me! And over
her attendant animal's pricked yellow ears she would say, "He
looks as if he were pulling on a pair of gloves!" (Yes, this was
her observation.) And then: "He must have a terrible temper!"
"But why? Why do you think so?" "Why? Well, of course, all
that control, everything so neat and clean, he must burst out
somewhere." And, once, "If he has a mistress"—the use of the
old-fashioned word was deliberate, part of the act—"then she
would have to be someone with a bad reputation, someone
rather awful, or *he* would have to think she was, or other people would have to think so even if he didn't. Because he would
have to feel wicked, don't you see?" Well, of course she was
right.

I found myself making excuses to sit there, to hear what

she would come out with. But I was reluctant, too, watching the knife being slipped in so neatly, so precisely, and again and again.

Of Janet White, a girl of about her age: "She'll spend her life looking for someone like Daddy, but where will she find him. I mean *now*—he won't exist." She meant, of course, the general break-up of things, times which were not conducive to the production of professors with very clean white shirts and a secret passion for the unrespectable—since respectability itself was sentenced to death, and with it the distinctions his secret needs must feed on. The Professor she called the White Rabbit. His daughter she called Daddy's Girl, making the point that in doing so she was of course describing herself: "What else, after all?" When I suggested that she might enjoy making a friend of Janet, she said, "What, me and her?"

Most of the day she lolled in a large chair that she pulled up for the purpose: a child, presenting herself as one. One could almost see the white socks on her plump well-turned legs, the bow in her hair. But what one really did see was different. She wore jeans and a shirt she had ironed that morning whose top two buttons were undone. Her hair was now parted in the middle, and at a stroke she was turned into a young beauty: yes, already, there she was.

And, as if in acknowledgement of this step forward into vulnerability, now her worst, or best, comments were for the boys who went past: this one's way of walking, which she knew represented an uncertainty about himself; that one's flashy way of dressing; the other one's bad skin, or unkempt hair. These unattractive grubs represented a force, an imperative, which there was no way of evading, and like a girl on a too high swing she was shrieking in thrilled terror.

She was dreadful in her accuracy. She depressed me—oh,

for many reasons; my own past being one of them. Yet she did not suspect this, she really did believe—so the bright manner, her confident glances at me said—that she was, as usual, "paying her way"; and this time by her perspicacity. She simply could not let anyone pass without swallowing them, and regurgitating them covered in her slime: the clever child, the one who could not be deceived, who could not have anything put over on her—who had been applauded for being like this, had been taught it.

And yet I came into the room once and saw her talking through the window with Janet White: she was earnest, warm, apparently sincere. If she did not like Janet White, she intended Janet White to like her. Infinite promises were made by both girls on the line of joint forays into the markets, visits, a walk. And when Janet went off, smiling because of the warmth she had absorbed from Emily, Emily said, "She's heard her parents talking about me, and now she'll report back." True enough, of course.

The point was that there wasn't anybody who came near her, into her line of sight, who was not experienced by her as a threat. This *was* how her experience, whatever that had been, had "set" her. I found I was trying to put myself in her place, tried to be her, to understand how it was that people must pass and repass sharply outlined by her need to criticise—to defend; and found I was thinking that this was only what everyone did, what I did, but there was something in her which enlarged the tendency, had set it forth, exaggerated. For of course, when someone new approaches us, we are all caution; we take that person's measure. A thousand incredibly rapid measurements and assessments go on, putting him, her, in an exact place, to end in the silent judgement: yes, this one's for me; no, we have nothing in common; no, he,

she, is a threat. . . . Watch out! Danger! And so on. But it was
not until Emily heightened it all for me that I realised what a
prison we were all in, how impossible it was for any one of us
to let a man or a woman or a child come near without the
defensive inspection, the rapid, sharp, cold analysis. But the
reaction was so fast, such a habit—probably the first ever taught
us by our parents—that we did not realise how much we were
in its grip.

"Look how she walks," Emily would say; "look at that
fat old woman." (The woman, of course, was about forty-five
or fifty; she might even be thirty!) "When she was young, people said she had a sexy walk—'Oh, what a sexy little wriggle
you have there; ooh, you sexy thing, you!' " And her parody
was horrible because of its accuracy: the woman, the wife of a
former stockbroker who had become a junk-dealer, and who
lived on the floor above, was given to a hundred little winsome
tricks of mouth and eyes and hips. This is what Emily saw of
her: it was what everybody must see first of her; and on these
tricks she was likely to be judged by most people. It was
impossible not to hear Emily without feeling one's whole
being, one's sense of oneself, lowered, drained. It was an assault on one's vitality: listening to her was to acknowledge the
limits we all live inside.

I suggested she might like to go to school—"for something
to do," I added hastily as I saw her quizzical look. This look
was not measured: it was her genuine reaction. So I was
catching a glimpse of what I had needed for some time: to
know what she thought of me, made of me—it was tolerance.

She said, "But what's the point?"

What was the point? Most schools had given up the
attempt of teaching; they had become—for the poorer people,
at least—extensions of the army, of the apparatus for keeping

the population under control. There were still schools for the children of the privileged class, the administrators and over-seers. Janet White went to one of them. But I thought too much of Emily to offer to send her to one, even if I was able to get a place for her. It was not that the education there was bad. It was irrelevant. It merited—a quizzical look.

"Not much point, I agree. And I suppose we won't be here long, anyway."

"Where do you think you'll go, then?"

This broke my heart: her forlorn isolation had never shown itself so sharply; she had spoken tentatively, even deli-cately, as if she had no right to ask, as if she had no right to my care, my protection—no share in my future.

Because of my emotion, I was more definite about my plans than I felt. I had, in fact, often wondered if a certain family I had known in north Wales would shelter me. They were good farming folk—yes, that is exactly the measure of my fantasies about them. "Good farming folk" was how safety, refuge, peace—utopia—shaped itself in very many peo-ple's minds in those days. But I did know Mary and George Dolgelly, had been familiar with their farm, had visited their guesthouse, open through the summers. If I made my way there, I might perhaps live there for a while? I was handy, liked to live simply, was as much at home out of cities as in them. . . . Of course, these qualifications belonged these days to large numbers of people, particularly the young, who could increasingly turn their hands to any job that needed doing. I did not imagine the Dolgellys would find me a prize. But at least they would not, I believed, find me a burden. And a child? Or, rather, a young girl? An attractive, challenging girl? Well, they had children of their own. . . . You can see that my thoughts had been pretty conventional, not very inventive. I talked to Emily, on these lines, while she listened, her sour little smile slowly giving way to amusement. But amusement concealed from politeness: I could not yet bring myself to believe that it was affection. She knew this fantasy for what it was; yet she enjoyed it, as I did. She asked me to describe the farm: I had once spent a week there, camping on a moor, with silvery water in little channels on a purple hillside. I took a can to Mary and George every morning for new milk, buying at the same time a loaf of their homemade bread. An idyll. I developed it, let it gather detail. We would take rooms in the guesthouse, and Emily would "help with the chickens"—a storybook touch, that. We would eat at the guesthouse table, a long wooden table. There was an old-fashioned stove in a recess. Stews and soups would simmer there, real food, and we would eat as much as we liked—no, that was not realistic, but as much as we needed—of real bread, real cheese, fresh vegetables, perhaps even, sometimes, a little good meat. There would be the smell of herbs from the bunches hanging to dry. The girl listened to all this, and I could not keep my eyes off her face, where the knowing sharp little smile alternated with her need to shield *me* from my inexperience, my sheltered condition! Stronger than anything else was something she was quite unconscious of, would certainly destroy all evidence of, if she knew she was betraying weakness. Stronger than the tricks, the need to please and to buy, the painful obedience, was this: a hunger, a need, a pure thing, which made her face lose its hard brightness, her eyes their defensiveness. She was a passion of longing. For what? Well, that is not so easy; it never is! But I recognised it, knew it, and talk of the farm in the Welsh hills did as well as anything to bring it out, to make it shine there: good bread, uncontaminated water from a deep well, fresh vegetables; love, kindness,

the deep shelter of a family. And so we talked about the farm,
our future, hers and mine, like a fable where we would walk
hand in hand, together. And then "life" would begin, life as it
ought to be, as it had been promised—by whom? When?
Where?—to everybody on this earth.

□   □   □

This idyllic time—of not more than a few days, in fact—
came abruptly to an end. One warm afternoon I looked out and
saw under the plane trees of the opposite pavement about
sixty young people, and recognised them as a pack of travellers
on their way through the city. This recognition was not always
easy, unless there were as many as this, for if you saw two or
three or four of such a troop separated from the others, you
might think they were students, who still—though there
weren't many of them—were to be seen in our city. Or they
could be the sons and daughters of ordinary people. Seen together, they were instantly unmistakable. Why? No, not only
that a mass of young people in these days could mean nothing
else. They had relinquished individuality, that was the point,
individual judgement and responsibility, and this showed in a
hundred ways, not least by one's instinctive reaction in an
encounter with them, which was always a sharp apprehension,
for one knew that in a confrontation—if it came to that—there
would be a pack judgement. They could not stand being alone
for long; the mass was their home, their place of self-recogni-
tion. They were like dogs coming together in a park or a
waste place. The sweet doggie belonging to the matron (her
smart voluminous coiffure a defence against the fear visible in

her pet, whose coat is an old lady's thin curls showing the
aged pink scalp but sheltered by a home-knitted scarlet wool
coat); the great Afghan, made to range forty miles a day without feeling it, shut it into his little house, his little garden; the
mongrel, bred from survivors; the spaniel, by nature a hunting dog—all these dear family companions, Togo and Bonzo
and Fluff and Wolf, having sniffed each other's bums and es-
tablished precedence, off they go, a pack, a unit. . . . This description is true of course of any group of people of any age
anywhere, if their roles are not already defined for them in
an institution. The gangs of "kids" were only showing the way
to their elders, who soon copied them; a "pack of youngsters"
nearly always, and increasingly, included older people, even
families, but the label remained. That is how people spoke of
the moving hordes—this last word at least was accurate before
the end, when it seemed as if a whole population were on the
move.

On this afternoon, with the trees above them heavy and
full, the sun making a festival—it was September, and still
warm—the pack settled down on the pavement, building a big
fire and arranging their possessions in a heap with a guard
stationed by it: two young boys armed with heavy sticks. The
whole area had emptied, as always happened. The police were
not to be seen: the authorities could not cope with this problem
and did not want to; they were happy to be rid of these gangs
who were in the process of taking elsewhere the problems they
raised. Every ground-floor window for miles around was closed
and the curtains drawn, but faces could be seen packing all the
higher windows of the blocks around us. The young people
stood around the fire in groups, and some couples had their
arms around each other. A girl played a guitar. The smell of
roasting meat was strong, and no one liked to think too much

about it. I wondered if Hugo was safe. I had not become fond
of this animal, but I was worried for Emily's sake. Then I
realised she was not in the living-room or the kitchen. I
knocked on her bedroom door, and opened it: the piled stuffy
nest of bedclothes she crept into for shelter against the world
was there, but she was not, and Hugo was not. Now I remembered that in the mass of young people was a young girl in
tight jeans and a pink shirt who was like Emily. But it had
been Emily, and from the window, I watched her. She stood
near the fire, a bottle in her hand, laughing—one of the gang,
the crowd, the team, the pack. Standing close against her legs,
fearful for himself, was the yellow animal: he had been hidden
by the press of the crowd. I saw she was shouting, arguing. She
retreated, her hand on Hugo's head. Slowly she backed away,
and then turned and ran, the animal bounding beside her:
to see him thus even momentarily was a painful reminder of
his power, his capacity, his range, now feebled by the little
rooms that held his life and his movements. A great shout of
raucous laughter went up from the young people; and from
this it was evident they had been teasing her about Hugo. They
had not really intended to kill him; they had been pretending
that they would; she had believed them. All this meant they
had not considered her as one of themselves, even potentially.
Yet there were children as young as she among them. She had
not challenged them as a child, no; but as a young girl, an
equal—that must have been it—and they had not accepted her.
All this came into my mind, had been reasoned out by me, by
the time she came into the living-room, white, trembling, terrified. She sat down on the floor and put her arms around her
Hugo, and hugged him close, swaying a little, back and forth,
saying, or singing, or sobbing, "Oh, no, no, no, dear Hugo, I
wouldn't, I couldn't, I wouldn't let them; don't be so fright-

ened." For he trembled as much as she did. He had his head on her shoulder, in their usual way of mutual comfort at such times.

But, in a moment, seeing I was there and that I had understood her rejection by the adult group she had challenged, she went red, she became angry. She pushed Hugo away and stood up, her face struggling for control. She became smiling and hard, and she laughed and said, "They are quite fun, really; I don't see why people say such nasty things about them." She went to the window to watch them out there, lifting the bottles to their mouths, passing around hunks of food as they shared their meal. Emily was subdued: perhaps she was even afraid, wondering how she could have gone out to them at all. Yet every one of us, the hundreds of people at our windows, knew that, watching them, we were examining our own possibilities, our future.

Soon, without looking at me, Emily pushed Hugo into her bedroom and shut the door, and she was off out of the flat and across the road again. Now the light of the fire made a tight bright space under the singeing trees. All the lower windows were dark but reflected the blaze or a cold gleam of light from a half-moon that stood between two towers of flats. The upper windows were full of heads outlined against varying kinds and degrees of light. But some of the ordinary citizens had already joined the young people, curious to find out where they had come from, where they were going; Emily was not the only one. I must confess that I had more than once visited an encampment for an evening. Not in this part of the town—no, I was fearful of my neighbours, of their condemnation—but I had seen faces I knew from my own neighbourhood: we were all doing the same, from the same calculation.

I was not fearful for what might happen to Emily if she behaved sensibly. If she did not, then I planned to cross the street and rescue her. I watched all night. Sometimes I was able to see her, sometimes not. Most of the time she was with a group of boys younger than the rest. She was the only girl, and she did behave foolishly, challenging them, asserting herself. But they were all drunk, and she was only one of the many ingredients of their intoxication.

There were people lying asleep on the pavement, their heads on a bundled sweater or on their forearms. They slept uncaring while the others milled about. This careless sleep, confident that the others would not tread on them, that they would be protected, said more than anything could about the kind of toughness these youngsters had acquired, the trust they had for each other. But general sleep was not what had been planned. The fire had died down. It would soon be morning. I saw that they were all gathering to move on. I had a bad half-hour wondering if Emily would leave with them. But after some embraces, loud and ribald, like the embraces and the jesting of tarts and soldiers when a regiment is moving off, and after she had run along beside them on the pavement for a few yards, she came slowly back—no, not to me, I knew better than to think that, but to Hugo. As she came in, her face was visible for a moment in the light from the corridor, a lonely sorrowful face, and not at all the face of a child. But by the time she had reached the living-room the mask was on. "That was a nice evening, say what you like," she remarked. I had not said anything, and I said nothing now. "Apart from eating people, they are very nice, I think," she said, with an exaggerated yawn. "And do they eat people?" "Well, I didn't ask, but I'd expect so, wouldn't you?" She opened the door to her little room, and Hugo came out, his green eyes watchful on her face, and she said to him, "It's all right, I haven't done anything you wouldn't have done, I promise you." And with this unhappy remark, and a hard little laugh, she went off, saying over her shoulder, "I could do worse than go off with them one of these days, that's what I think. They enjoy themselves, at least."

Well, I preferred that good night to many others we had exchanged when at ten o'clock she would cry, "Oh, it's my bedtime, off I go," and a dutiful good night kiss hung between us, a ghost, like the invisible white gloves of Professor White.

It happened that during that early autumn, day after day, fresh gangs came through. And, day after day, Emily was with them. She did not ask if she could. And I wasn't going to forbid her, for I knew she would not obey me. I had no authority. She was not my child. We avoided a confrontation. She was there whenever the pavements opposite were crowded and the fire blazing. On two occasions she was very drunk, and once she had a torn skirt and bite marks on her neck. She said, "I suppose you think I've lost my virginity? Well, I haven't, though it was a close thing, I grant you." And then the cold little addition, her signature, "If it matters, which I doubt."

"I think it matters," I said.

"Oh, do you? Well, you are an optimist, I suppose. Something of that kind. What do you think, Hugo?"

That sequence of travelling gangs came to an end. The pavements up and down the street were blackened and cracked with the fires that had been blazing there for so many nights, the leaves of the plane trees hung limp and blasted, bones and bits of fur and broken glass lay everywhere, the waste lot behind was trampled and filthy. Now the police materialised, were busy taking notes and interviewing people.

The cleaners came around. The pavements went back to
normal. Everything went back to normal for a time, and the
ground-floor windows had lights in them at night.

It was about then I understood that the events on the
pavements and what went on between me and Emily might
have a connection with what I saw on my visits behind the
wall.

Moving through the tall quiet white walls, as imperma-
nent as theatre sets, knowing that the real inhabitant was there,
always there just behind the next wall, to be glimpsed on the
opening of the next door or the one beyond that, I came on a
room—long, deep-ceilinged, once a beautiful room—which I
recognised, which I knew (from where, though?), and it was
in such disorder I felt sick and was afraid. The place looked
as if savages had been in it; as if soldiers had bivouacked there.
The chairs and sofas had been deliberately slashed and jabbed
with bayonets or knives, stuffing was spewing out everywhere,
brocade curtains had been ripped off the brass rods and left
in heaps. The room might have been used as a butcher's shop:
there were feathers, blood, bits of offal. I began cleaning it. I
laboured, used many buckets of hot water, scrubbed, mended. I
opened tall windows to an eighteenth-century garden where
plants grew in patterns of squares among low hedges. Sun and
wind were invited into that room and cleaned it. I was by myself all the time, yet did not feel myself to be. Then it was done.
The old sofas and chairs stood there repaired and clean. The
curtains were stacked for the cleaners. I walked around in it
for a long time, for it was a room large enough for pacing; and
I stood at the windows, seeing hollyhocks and damask roses,
smelling lavender, roses, rosemary, verbena, conscious of memories assaulting me, claiming, insinuating. One was from my
"real" life, for it was nagging and tugging at me that the pave-

ments where the fires had burned and the trees had scorched were part of the stuff and the substance of this room. But there was the tug of nostalgia for the room itself, the life that had been lived there, that would continue the moment I had left. And for the garden, whose every little turn or corner I knew in my bones. Above all, for the inhabitant who was somewhere near, probably watching me; who, when I had left, would walk in and nod approval at the work of cleaning I had done and then perhaps go out to walk in the garden.

What I found next was in a very different setting: above all, in a different atmosphere. It was the first of the "personal" experiences. This was the word I used for them from the start. And the atmosphere was unmistakable always, as soon as I entered whatever scene it was. That is, between the feeling or texture or mood of the scenes which were not "personal"—like, for instance, the long quiet room that had been so devastated, or any of the events, no matter how wearying or difficult or discouraging, that I saw in this or that setting—between these and the "personal" scenes a world lay; the two kinds, "personal" (though not necessarily, to me) and the other, existed in spheres quite different and separated. One, the "personal," was instantly to be recognised by the air that was its prison, by the emotions that were its creatures. The impersonal scenes might bring discouragement or problems that had to be solved —like the rehabilitation of walls or furniture, cleaning, putting order into chaos—but in that realm there was a lightness, a freedom, a feeling of possibility. Yes, that was it, the space and the knowledge of the possibility of alternative action. One could refuse to clean that room, clear that patch of earth; one could walk into another room altogether, choose another scene. But to enter the "personal" was to enter a prison, where nothing could happen but what one saw happening, where the air was tight and limited, and above all where time was a strict unalterable law and long—oh, my God, it went on, and on and on, minute by decreed minute, with no escape but the slow wearing away of one after another.

It was again a tall room, but this time square and without grace, and there were tall but heavy windows, with dark red velvet curtains. A fire burned, and in front of it was a strong fireguard, like a wire meat cover. On this were airing a great many thick or flimsy napkins, baby's napkins of the old-fashioned sort, and many white vests and binders, long and short dresses, robes, jackets, little socks. An Edwardian layette, emitting that odour which is not quite scorch but near to it: heated, airless materials. There was a rocking horse. Alphabet books. A cradle with muslin flounces, minute blue and green flowers on white. . . . I realised what a relief the colour was, for everything was white—white clothing, white cot and cradle and covers and blankets and sheets and baskets. A white-painted room. A little white clock that would have been described in a catalogue as a Nursery Clock. White. The clock's tick was soft and little and incessant.

A small girl of about four sat on a hearthrug, with the clothing that was set to air between her and the flames. She wore a dark blue velvet dress. She had dark hair parted on one side and held by a large white ribbon. She had intensely serious, already defensive dark hazel eyes.

On the bed was a baby, being bundled for the night. The baby was chuckling. A nurse or attendant hung over the baby; but only a broad white back was visible. The little girl's look as she watched the loving nurse bending over the brother was enough; it said everything. But there was more: another figure, immensely tall, large, and powerful, came into the room; it was a personage all ruthless energy, and she, too, bent over the baby, and the two females joined in a ceremony of loving while the baby wriggled and responded and cooed. And the little girl watched. Everything around her was enormous: the room so large, warm, and high, the two women so tall and strong and disliking, the furniture daunting and difficult, the clock with its soft hurrying which told everyone what to do, was obeyed by everyone, consulted, constantly watched.

Being invited into this scene was to be absorbed into child-space; I saw it as a small child might—that is, enormous and implacable—but at the same time I kept with me my knowledge that it was tiny and implacable—because petty, unimportant. This was a tyranny of the unimportant, of the mindless. Claustrophobia, airlessness, a suffocation of the mind, of aspiration. And all endless, for this was child-time, where one day's end could hardly be glimpsed from its beginning, ordered by the hard white clock. Each day was like something to be climbed, like the great obdurate chairs, a bed higher than one's head, obstacles and challenges overcome by the aid of large hands that gripped and pulled and pushed—hands which, seen at work on that baby, seemed to be tender and considerate. The baby was high in the air, held up in the nurse's arms. The baby was laughing. The mother wanted to take the baby from the nurse, but the nurse held tight and said, "Oh, no, this one—this is *my* baby, he's my baby." "Oh, no, Nurse," said the strong tower of a mother, taller than anything in the room, taller than the big nurse, almost as high as the ceiling: "Oh, no," she said, smiling but with her lips tight, "he's *my* baby." "No, this is my baby," said the nurse, now rocking and crooning the infant, "he's my darling baby, but the other one, she's your baby. Emily is yours, Madam." And she turned her back on the mother in a show of emotional independence, while she loved and rocked the baby. At which the mother smiled, a smile different from the other, and not understood by the little girl, except that it led to her being pulled up roughly on the mother's hand, and told, "Why aren't you undressed? I told you to get undressed." And there began a rapid uncomfortable scrambling and pushing; she was trying to remain steady on her feet while layers of clothes were pulled off her. First the blue velvet dress of which she was proud, because it suited her—she had been told so by voices of all kinds insisting against each other high over her head—but it had many little buttons up the inside of her arm and down her back, each one taking so long to undo while the big fingers hurt and bruised. Then off came the petticoat, quite fast but scratching at her chin, then long white tights too big for her which released a warm likeable smell into the air: the mother noticed it and made a grimace. "And now into bed with you," she said as she hastily pulled down a white nightdress over the child's head.

Emily crept into her bed near the window, hauling herself up by the head-rail, for to her it was a big bed; and she lifted a corner of the heavy red velvet to look out at the stars. At the same time, she watched the two large people, the mother and the nurse, tending the baby. Her face was old and weary. She seemed to understand it all, to have foreseen it, to be living through it because she had to, feeling it as a thick heaviness all around her—Time, through which she must push herself till she could be free of it. For none of them could help themselves—not the mother, that feared and powerful woman; not the nurse, bad-tempered because of her life; not the baby, for whom she, the little girl, already felt a passion of love that melted her, made her helpless. And she, the child, could not help herself, either, not at all; and when the mother said— in her impatient rough way, which came out as a sort of gaiety,

a courage that even then the child recognised as a demand on
her compassion—"Emily, you should lie down. Off to sleep
with you," she lay down; and watched the two women taking
the baby off into another room from where could be heard a
man's voice, the father's. A ceremony of good night, and she
was excluded: they had forgotten she had not been taken to
say good night to her father. She turned herself over, back
to the hot white room, where the red flames pulsed out heat,
filled the heavy white clothes on the bars with hot smells,
made red shadows in the caves behind the edges of the red
curtains, made a prickling heat start up all over her under
the heavy bedclothes. She took hold of the dangling red tassels
on the curtains, brought them close to her, and lay pulling
them, pulling them. . . .

   This small child was of course the Emily who had been
given into my care, but I did not understand for some days
that I had been watching a scene from her childhood (but that
was impossible, of course, since no such childhood existed these
days; it was obsolete): a scene, then, from her memory, or her
history, which had formed her. . . . I was with her one morning, and some movement she made told me what should have
been obvious. Then I kept glancing at that young face, such a
troubling mixture of the child and the young girl, and could
see in it her solitary four-year-old self. Emily. I wondered if
she remembered anything of her memories, or experiences, that
were being "run" like a film behind my living-room wall,
which at the moment—the sun lighting a slant of air and the
white paint where the flowery pattern of the paper maintained
its frail but stubborn being—was a transparent screen: this was
one of the moments when the two worlds were close together,
when it was easy to remember that it was possible simply to
walk through. I sat and looked at the wall, and fancied I heard

sounds that certainly were not part of "my" world at all: a
poker being energetically used in a grate, of small feet running,
a child's voice.

I wondered if I should say something to Emily, ask her
questions? But I did not dare; that was the truth. I was afraid
of her. It was my helplessness with her I feared.

She was wearing her old jeans that were much too tight
for her, a bulging little pink shirt.

"You ought to have some new clothes," I said.

"Why? Don't you think I look nice, then?" The awful
"brightness" of it; but there was dismay as well. . . . She
had gathered herself together, ready to withstand criticism.

"You look very nice. But you've grown out of those
clothes."

"Oh, dear, I didn't realise it was as bad as that."

And she took herself away from me and lay on the long
brown sofa with Hugo beside her. She was not actually sucking
her thumb, but she might just as well have been.

I ought to describe her attitude to me? But it is difficult. I
don't think she often saw me. When brought to me first by
that man, whoever he was, she saw an elderly person, saw me
clearly, sharp, minutely, in detail. But since then I don't think
she had for one moment, not in all the weeks she had been
with me, seen more than an elderly person, with the character-
istics to be expected of one. She had no idea of course of the
terror I felt on her account, the anxiety, the need to protect.
She did not know that the care of her had filled my life, water
soaking a sponge . . . but did I have the right to complain?
Had I not, like all the other adults, talked of "the youth," "the
youngsters," "the kids," and so on. Did I not still, unless I
made an effort not to? Besides, there is little excuse for the
elderly to push the young away from them into compartments

of their minds labelled: "This I do not understand," or "This I will not understand," for every one of them has been young. . . . Should I be ashamed of writing this commonplace when so few middle-aged and elderly people are able to vivify it by practice? When so few are able to acknowledge their memories? The old have been young; the young have never been old—these remarks or some like them have been in a thousand diaries, books of moral precepts, commonplace books, proverbs, and so on, and what difference have they made? Well, I would say not very much. . . . Emily saw some dry, controlled, distant old person. I frightened her, representing to her that unimaginable thing, old age. But for my part, she, her condition, was as close to me as my own memories.

When she went to lie on the sofa, her back to me, she was sulking. She was making use of me to check her impulse to step forward away from childhood into being a girl, a young girl with clothes and mannerisms and words regulated precisely to that condition.

Her conflict was great, and so her use of me was inordinate and tiresome, and it all went on for some weeks, while she complained that I criticised her appearance, and it was my fault she was going to have to spend money on clothes, and that she did or did not like how she looked—that she did not want to wear nothing but trousers and shirts and sweaters for the whole of her life, and wanted "something decent to wear at last," but that since my generation had made such a mess of everything, hers had nothing interesting to wear, people her age were left with ancient fashion magazines and dreams of the delicious and dead past. . . . And so it went, on and on.

And now it wasn't only that she was older and her body showing it: she was putting on weight. She would lie all day on the sofa with her yellow dog-like cat, or cat-like dog; she would lie hugging him and petting him and stroking him; she would suck sweets and eat bread and jam and fondle the animal and daydream. Or she sat at the window making her sharp little comments, eating. Or she would supply herself with stacks of bread and jam, cake, apples, and arrange a scene in the middle of the floor with old books and magazines, lying face down with Hugo sprawled across the back of her thighs: there she would read and dream and eat her way through a whole morning, a whole day, days at a time.

It drove me quite wild with irritation: yet I could remember doing it myself.

Suddenly she would leap up and go to the mirror and cry out, "Oh, dear, I'll be getting so fat you'll think I'm even more ugly than you do now!" Or, "I won't be able to get into any clothes even when you do let me buy some new ones. I know you don't really want me to have new ones, you just say so; you think I'm being frivolous and heartless, when so many people can't even eat."

I could only reiterate that I would be delighted if she bought herself some clothes. She could go to the secondhand markets and shops, as most people did. Or, if she liked, she could go to the real shops—just this once. For buying clothes or materials in the shops was by that time a status symbol; the shops were really used only by the administering class, by—as most people called them—the Talkers. I knew she was attracted by the idea of actually going to a real shop. But she ignored the money I had left in a drawer for her, and went on eating and dreaming.

I was out a good deal, busy on that common occupation, gathering news. For while I had, like everyone else, a radio, while I was a member of a newspaper circle—shortage of newsprint made it necessary for groups of people to buy newspapers and journals in common and circulate them—I, like everyone else, looked for news, real news, where people congregated in the streets, in bars and pubs and teahouses. All over the city were these groups of people, moving from one place to another, pub to teahouse to bar to outside the shops that still sold televisions. These groups were like an additional organ burgeoning on the official organs of news; all the time, new groups or couples or individuals added themselves to a scene, stood listening, mingling, offering what they themselves had heard—news having become a sort of currency—giving, in exchange for rumour and gossip, gossip and rumour. Then we moved on, and stopped; moved on and stopped again, as if movement itself could allay the permanent unease we all felt. News gathered in this way was often common talk days or even weeks before it was given official life in the newscasts. Of course it was often inaccurate. But then all news is inaccurate. What people were trying to do, in their continual moving about and around, nosing out news, taking in information, was to isolate residues of truth in rumour, for there was nearly always that. We felt we had to have this precious residue: it was our due, our right. Having it made us feel safer and gave us identity. Not getting it, or enough of it, deprived us, made us anxious.

This is how we saw it then. Now I think something different: that what we were doing was talking. We talked. Just like those people above us who spent their lives in their eternal and interminable conferences, talking about what was happening, what should happen, what they fondly hoped they could make happen—but of course never did—we talked. We called them the Talkers . . . and ourselves spent hours of every day talking and listening to talk.

Mostly, of course, we wanted to know what was happening

in the territories to the east and to the south—referred .to as "out there" or "down there"—because we knew that what happened there would sooner or later affect us. We had to know what gangs were approaching, or rumoured to be approaching—gangs which, as I've said, were not all "kids" and "youngsters" now, were made up of every kind and age of person, were more and more tribes, were the new social unit. We had to know what shortages were expected or might be abating; if another suburb had decided to turn its back entirely on gas, electricity, and oil and revert to candle-power and ingenuity; if a new rubbish dump had been found, and if so, could ordinary people get access to its riches; where there were shops that might have hides or old blankets or rose hips for vitamin syrups, or recycled plastic objects, or metal things like sieves and saucepans, or whatever it was, whatever might be cast up from the dead time of plenty.

Of course, such contriving and patching and making do began to parallel our ordinary living, our affluence and waste and overeating, at a very early stage, long before the time of which I am writing now. We were all experts at making a great deal out of very little, even while we all still had a lot, and were still being incited by advertisements to spend and use and discard.

Sometimes I left Emily—fearful, of course, for what might happen in my absence, but thinking the risk worth it—to make trips a good way out from the city, to villages, farms, other towns. These might take two or three days, since the trains and buses were so infrequent and unreliable, and the cars, nearly all of them used by officialdom, so reluctant to offer lifts because of the fear of ordinary people felt by the official class. I walked, having rediscovered the uses of my feet, like most people.

One day I returned to the flat and to Emily with half a dozen sheepskins. Other things as well, which I put away in cupboards and hiding places with supplies of all kinds for future and still only partly imagined contingencies, but it was the skins that were important, since they started her off on a new phase of her development. At first she pretended to ignore them. Then I saw her standing in front of a long mirror I had in the hall, or lobby, and she was pinning them on her. She seemed to be aiming at a savage-princess effect, but as soon as she knew I had noticed and was interested, she returned to her place on the sofa with Hugo, returned to her daydream which excluded the time we were in fact living through. Yet I believe she was intrigued by the business of survival, its resources and tricks and little contrivances. I remember that it was at that time she took pleasure in creating a dish of dumplings and gravy, using nothing but some old onions, withering potatoes, and herbs, presenting it with a flourish like a chef's. She liked the markets where she tracked down things I would never have bothered myself with. She enjoyed—what I always found irritating and could not help contrasting with the simplicities and efficiencies of the past—building up the fire to heat water for washing and cooking. She scolded me for being prepared to use the stocks of wood I had, and insisted on running out to some deserted building to bring back old skirting boards and suchlike, which she proceeded to split, using an axe skilfully then and there on the carpet, shielding this with old rags from even worse wear than it had suffered already. Yes, she was very handy, and this said everything about her experiences before she had come to me. And she knew I was watching and drawing my conclusions; and this sent her back to the sofa, for her need to be secret, her need not to be understood and found out, was stronger, even now, than anything. Yet I was comforted, seeing her skills and her resources, and the heavy load of foreboding I carried about with me because of her future was lightened: how could this heavy, dreaming, erratic child, so absorbed in herself, in fantasy, in the past, survive what we would all have to survive? And I began to realise just how dark a foreboding it was, how I had come to watch and grieve over her, how sharp was my anxiety when she was out in empty buildings and waste lots. "Why do you think I can't look after myself?" she cried, in a rage of irritation, though of course—being Emily and so instructed in the need to please, to placate—she smiled and tried to hide it: the real irritation, her real emotions, she must hide and dim, while her pretend angers and sulks, the adolescent's necessary playacting, were on display all the time.

Now I was thankful Hugo was there. He was not a difficult animal (I nearly said person!) to share a home with. He did not seem to sleep much; he kept watch. I believe this was how he saw his function: he was to look after her. He preferred Emily to feed him, but would eat if I put his food down. He wished to be her only friend and love; yet was courteous with me—I am afraid that is the only word for it. He looked forward to his trip out of doors on his heavy chain in the evenings, was disappointed if Emily could not take him, went obligingly with me. He ate the nasty substances that were being sold as dog food, but preferred the remains from our plates and showed that he did.

Not that there was ever much left: Emily ate and ate, and she had taken to wearing her little shirts outside her bursting trousers. She stood glooming at herself in front of the mirror, her jaws moving over sweets or bread. I said nothing; I made a point of saying nothing, even when she challenged me: "It suits me to be fat, don't you think?" Or: "I'll make better eating when cooked for the feast." But whatever she said, however she joked, she ate. She lay on the floor, her hand automatically conveying bread, more bread, cake, potato mixtures, fruit dumplings to her mouth, while her eyes followed the lines of print in some old book she had picked up but would soon let drop while she stared in front of her, her eyes glazed. Hour after hour. Day after day. Sometimes she would jump up to make herself some beverage or other, and offer me a cup; then she forgot me. Her mouth was always in movement, chewing, tasting, absorbed in itself, so that she seemed all mouth, and everything else in her was subordinated to that; it seemed as if even the intake of words through her eyes was another form of eating, and her daydreaming a consumption of material, which was bloating her as much as her food.

And then, suddenly, it all went into reverse. Of course it did not seem sudden at the time. It is now, looking back, that it is all so obvious: even, I am afraid, banal and mechanical, as the inevitable does seem—in retrospect.

Some youths from our blocks of flats took to hanging about on the opposite pavement and the waste lot, under the scorched trees. These youths were sharing in lost glory and adventure: memories of the time when migrating tribes had lit fires and feasted there. They pointed out to each other the blackened parts of the pavement, told and retold episodes from the epic. At first there were two or three, then half a dozen, then . . . Emily had forsaken her dreaming to watch them. Not that you could make out from her face anything but scorn of them. I remember I felt pity for the raucous adolescent boys, so desperately wanting to be noticed and looked at, who were so forlorn and unappetising in their lumpish bodies; pity for her, the fat girl looking out of her window, the princess in disguise. I marvelled that such a short time, a few years, would

transform these grubs into beauties. But I was wrong: time
had so speeded up that years were not needed any longer. . . .
One evening Emily sauntered out and stood in front of the
building with a look like a jeer, while her body pleaded and
demanded. The boys ignored her. Then they made some comments about her figure. She came indoors, sat thoughtfully in
her sofa corner for some hours—and stopped eating.

She lost weight fast. She was living on herb teas and
yeast extracts. And now I watched the reverse process, a shape
emerging whole and clear while increments of lard melted
away around it.

I began to remonstrate: you must eat something, you
should set yourself a proper diet. But she did not hear me. I
was distant from her need to make herself worthy of the
heroes of the pavement—quite a few of them now that the
days were lengthening and spring healed the scarred trees.

We were watching, though I still did not recognise this,
the birth of a gang, a pack, a tribe. It would be pleasant to be
able to say now that I was aware of the processes going on in
front of me. Now I judge myself to have been blind. How else
do things work always unless by imitation bred of the passion
to be like? All the processes of society are based on it, all
individual development. For some reason, it was something
that we seemed to have a conspiracy to ignore or not to mention, even while most single-mindedly engaged in it. There
was some sort of conspiracy of belief that people—children,
adults, everyone—grew by an acquisition of unconnected habits,
of isolated bits of knowledge, like choosing things off a
counter: "Yes, I'll have that one," or, "No, I don't want that
one!" But in fact people develop for good or for bad by swallowing whole other people, atmospheres, events, places—develop by admiration. Often enough unconsciously, of course.
We are the company we keep.

In front of my eyes, on that pavement, for weeks, for months, I could have watched, as in a textbook or a laboratory, the genesis, growth, and flowering of society's new unit. But I did no such thing, for I was absorbed in Emily, my concern for her. Those processes went on, and I observed them; details did stand out for me; I watched for the effects of this or that event on Emily. It is only now, looking back, I see what an opportunity I missed.

Emily was not the only young girl preparing herself to take her place as a woman among other women. Janet White, for instance: for a while, before her parents stopped her, Janet passed a dozen times a day before our windows in front of the jeering boys. There was a period when boys and girls, on opposite sides of the road, stood in hostile battalions exchanging taunts and abuse.

Then it was noticeable that they jeered less, stood more often in silence, or quietly talking among themselves, though always watching the other groups while pretending not to.

Inside the flat Emily remembered the sheepskins. Again she arranged them around her, belted them tight, swaggered about in them with her hair loose.

She came to me: "I found that sewing machine. Can I use it?"

"Of course. But don't you want to buy clothes? That thing is so old. It must be thirty-five years old."

"It works."

The money I had given her was still in the drawer. This she now took out and quickly, almost secretively, walked the five or six miles to the centre of the city where the big shops were with the goods for the official class, or for anyone who could afford them. Nearly always the same thing. She came back with some good cloth from the pre-crisis time. She came back with sewing cottons and a tape measure and scissors.

She also visited the secondhand shops and the market stalls, and
the floor of her room was heaped with loot, with booty. She
invited Janet White in from the pavement, having of course
first politely asked my permission, and the two nymphs
squeezed themselves into the tiny room, and chattered and
competed, and arranged their images this way and that before
the long mirror—a ritual which was repeated when Janet
White in her turn went off on her foray to capture materials
and old clothes . . . repeated in Janet's room along the corridor. And this led to her being forbidden the street and the
pleasures of the tribe and warned not to take Emily for a
friend. For Janet was destined differently. To tell the truth,
I did not realise how high the Whites were placed in the ad-
ministrative circles; but then, they were not the only official
family to half hide themselves in this way, living quietly in an
ordinary flat, apparently like everyone else, but with access to
sources of food, goods, clothes, transport denied to most.

Emily did not seem to mind Janet discarding her. There
followed a period of weeks when she was every bit as self-
absorbed as when she had been eating, dreaming, indolent, but
now she was full of energy and self-denial, at least for food,
and I watched, I watched endlessly, for I had never seen anything like this for concentration.

For if she, Emily, had gone inwards as much in this new
activity as she had when lazy and dreaming, at least now what
she felt herself to be was all visible, presented to me in the
shape of her fantastic costumes.

Her first self-portrait . . . she had found an old dress,
white with sprigs of pink flowers. Parts were stained and
worn. These she cut away. Bits of lace and tulle, beads, scarves
were added to and removed from a kaleidoscope garment that
changed with her needs. Most often it was a bride's dress. Then

it was a young girl's dress—that ambiguous declaration of
naïveté more usually made by a maturer vision than that
of the wearer, an eye that sees the fragility of certain types of
young girls' clothes as the expression of the evanescence of
that flesh. It was nightdress when she wore its transparency
over her naked body. It was evening dress, and sometimes when
she did not intend this, for a hardness in her, the watchfulness
of her defences, took away innocence from anything she wore,
so that she might have flowers in her hands and in her hair,
in an attempt at her version of Primavera, yet she had about her
the look of a woman who has calculated the exact amount of
flesh she will show at a dinner party. This dress was for me an
emotional experience. I was frightened by it. Again, this was
a question of my helplessness with her. I believed her capable
of going out on the pavement wearing it. Now I judge myself
to have been stupid: the elderly tend not to see—they have forgotten!—that hidden person in the young creature, the strongest
and most powerful member among the cast of characters in-
habiting an adolescent body, the self which instructs, chooses
experience—and protects.

And then, to see this creation at such a time of savagery
and anarchy, this archetype of a girl's dress—or, rather, this
composite of archetypes; the way this child, this little girl, had
found the materials for her dreams in the rubbish heaps of our
old civilisation, had found them, worked on them, and in spite
of everything had made her images of herself come to life . . .
but such old images, so indestructible, and so *irrelevant*—all
this was too much for me, and I retired from the scene, determined to say nothing, show nothing, betray nothing. And
it was lucky I did. She wore the thing about the flat, a naked
girl only just veiled; she wore it flauntingly, bashfully, dar-
ingly, fearfully; she was "trying on" not a dress but self-por-

traits, and I might as well not have been there; she took no
notice of me. Well, of course, the pressures on everyone's privacy had taught us how to absent ourselves into inner solitudes;
we were all adept at being with others and not being with
them.

But I really did not know whether to laugh or to cry;
I did a little of both—of course when she could not see me.
For she was so ludicrous, as well as so brave and resourceful,
with her straight, honest, hazel eyes, her English good-com-
rade's eyes, unsubtle, judging, wary; with her attempts at
make-up on a fresh little face languishing away there behind
harem veils, her body stiff in "seductive" poses. This dress
possessed her for weeks. Then one day she took scissors and
cut off the bottom in a gesture of derisive impatience: something had not worked, or had worked for her and it was all
over, not needed. She threw the jaded bundle into a drawer
and began on a new invention of herself.

There was a late, and prolonged, cold spell. There was
even a little snow. In my flat, warmth was a much-coaxed
visitor and, like everyone else, we were wearing almost as many
clothes indoors as we did out. Emily took the sheepskins and
made a long dramatic tunic. This she belted with some scarlet
chiffon, and she wore it over an old shirt she had taken from
my cupboard. Without asking. I cannot say how delighted I
was when she did this. It showed she felt she had some rights
with me, at last. The child's right to be naughty, for one; but
it was more than that: an elderly or a mature person finds
some young one simply taking something, a personal thing,
particularly if it is a strong expression or statement of a phase
of life (as a pink-sprigged white dress is for a young girl), and
what a release it is, a shock—cold water on shrinking flesh,
if you like—but a liberation. *This is more mine than yours,*

says the act of the theft; *more mine because I need it more; it fits my stage life better than it does yours; you have outgrown it. . . .* And perhaps the exhilaration it releases is even a hint of an event still in the future, that moment when the person sees in the eyes of people the statement—still unconscious, perhaps: *You can hand over your life now; you don't need it any longer; we will live it for you; please go.*

The shirt had been among my clothes for thirty years, had once been a sophisticated thing, was of fine green silk. Now it went under Emily's sheepskin swagger, and just as I was wrestling with the need to say, "For heaven's sake, you can't wear that brigand's outfit out of doors; it is an invitation to assault," she allowed the contraption to fall apart, for it was only tacked and pinned together, no more permanent than a daydream.

And so we went on. She did not go out of the flat, not in any of her fantasies; and I observed that they were becoming more utilitarian.

Chrysalis after chrysalis was outgrown, and then, because of her shame at having wasted so much, she asked abruptly and gracelessly but in her over-polite and *awful* way for some more money, and went off by herself to the markets. She came back with some secondhand clothes that in one giant's step took her from being a child with fantastic visions of herself into a girl—a woman, rather. She was thirteen then, not yet fourteen; but she might as well have been seventeen or eighteen, and it happened in an explosion of days. Now I thought that probably the heroes of the pavement would be beneath her; that she, a young woman, would demand what nature would in fact have chosen for her, a young man of seventeen, eighteen, even more.

But the crowd, the pack, the gang—not yet a tribe, but

on its way to being one—had suffered forced growth, as she
had. A few weeks had done it. While snow had bleached the
pavements and heightened the black of tree branches frilled
and dangling with new green—had shrunk away and returned
again—while Emily had mated herself in imagination with
romantic heroes and chief executives and harem tyrants, a
dozen or so young men had emerged from their disguises as
louts and yokels, and at evening stood around under the trees
swaggering in colourful clothes, and the girls of the neighbourhood had come out to join them. Now sometimes as many as
thirty or more young people were being watched in the lengthening afternoons of early spring from hundreds of windows.
By now it had dawned on the neighbourhood that a phenomenon we had believed could belong only to the regions
"out there" was being born before our eyes, in our own streets,
where until now it had seemed that at worst nothing could
happen but the passage of some alien migrations.

We heard that the same thing was to be observed in other
parts of our city. It was not only on our pavements that the
young people were gathering in admiration and then emula-
tion of the migrating tribes; and, while emulating, became.
We all knew, we understood, and it was spoken of in the tea-
shops and pubs and at all the usual gathering places: it was
discussed, making news, making things happen. We knew
that soon our young people would leave; we made the ritual
noises of wonder and alarm; but now it was happening, everyone knew it had been bound to happen, and we marvelled at
our lack of foresight—and at the short-sightedness of others,
whose neighbourhoods were still without this phenomenon
and who believed they were immune.

Emily began showing herself off. First from our window,
making sure she had been seen, and then on the pavement out-

side, strolling there as if unaware of the young people across
the road. This period took longer than I expected, or than
she needed to be accepted. I think, now it came to the point,
she was afraid of taking this big step away from shelter, from
childhood, from the freedom of fantasy: for now she looked
like the other girls and must behave and think like them. And
how did they look? Well, the key to the clothes of the migrating ones was of course practicality. It had to be: utility stylised.
Trousers, jackets, sweaters, and scarves, everything thick and
strong and warm. But from the markets, the rubbish dumps,
the old warehouses came what seemed an endless supply of
old "fashionable" clothes that could be adapted or, at any rate,
transformed into bits and pieces of all kinds. So what they
looked like was gipsies, of the old sort, and for the same
reason. They had to be warm and free to move; their feet
would have to carry them long distances. But an exuberancy
of fancy kept them colourful, and warm weather brought them
out like butterflies.

There came a day when Emily walked across the street
and added herself to the crowd there, as if it were quite easy
for her to do this. Almost at once she accepted a cigarette from
the boy who seemed to be the strongest personality there, allowed it to be lit for her, and smoked with ease. I had never
seen her smoke. She was there while the light faded out of the
sky around the tall buildings with their little glimmering
windows. She was there long afterwards. The young people
were a half-visible mass under the branches. They stood talking softly, smoking, drinking from bottles they kept lodged
in their jacket pockets; or they sat on the little parapet that
surrounded the paving of the nearest blocks of flats. That space
of pavements and waste lot, with the trees and the weeds—
bounded on one side by the little parapet, on the other by an

old wall—had become defined, like an arena or a theatre. The
crowds there had claimed it, shaped it: we would not again be
able to see that space as anything but where the tribe was
forming.

But Hugo was not there. She had hugged him, kissed him,
talked to him, whispered into his ugly yellow ears. But she
had left him.

He sat on a chair at the window and watched her, making
sure that the curtains concealed him.

Coming suddenly into the room, a stranger would have
to say, "That's a very yellow dog!" Then: "Is it a dog,
though?" What I saw of him, though Emily never did, for he
was turned to face her entrance from the moment she crossed
the street to come home, was a straw-yellow dog sitting with
its back to the room, absolutely still, hour after hour, its whip-
tail sticking out through the bars of the chair, all of him expressing a sad and watchful patience. A dog. A dog's emotions
—fidelity, humility, endurance. Seen thus from the back, Hugo
aroused the emotions most dogs do: compassion, discomfort, as
if for a kind of prisoner or slave. But then he would turn
his head and, expecting to see the warm abject lovingness of a
dog's eyes, fellow-feeling vanished away: this was no dog, half-
humanised. His strong green eyes blazed. Inhuman. Cat's eyes,
a genus foreign to man, not sorry and abject and pleading.
Cat's eyes in a dog's body—cat's eyes and face. This beast,
whose ugliness drew one's eyes as good looks do, so that I was
always finding myself staring at him, trying to come to terms
with him and understand the right he assumed to be there in
my life—this aberration, this freak, kept watch over Emily,
and with as much devotion as I did. And it was Hugo who was
hugged, caressed, loved when she returned at night smelling
of smoke, of drink, and full of the dangerous vitality she had

absorbed from the wild company she had been part of for so many hours.

She was with them now every day, from early afternoon until midnight and after; and I and the animal would be sitting behind the curtains, peering out at the dark, for there was only one street lamp, and nothing much could be seen of the crowd milling about out there, except the pallor of faces, little gleams and flashes as cigarettes were lit; nothing heard of their talking together until they laughed, or sang for a while, or when voices rose wildly in a quarrel—and at such times I could feel Hugo trembling and shrinking. But quarrels were soon quelled by general consent, a communal veto.

And when we knew Emily was coming back, both of us, Hugo and myself, would quickly leave our post and go to where we could be believed to be asleep, or at least not spying on her.

□   □   □

Throughout this period, whenever I was drawn in through the flowers and leaves submerged under half-transparent white paint, I found rooms disordered or damaged. I never saw who or what did it, or even caught a glimpse of the agent. It was seeming to me more and more that in inheriting this extension of my ordinary life, I had been handed, again, a task. Which I was not able to carry through. For no matter how I swept, picked up and replaced overturned chairs, tables, objects; scrubbed floors and rubbed down walls, whenever I re-entered the rooms after a spell away in my real life, all had to be done again. It was like what one reads of a poltergeist's

tricks. Already my entrance into that place was with a lowered
vitality, a sense of foreboding, instead of the lively and loving
anticipation I had felt on first being able to move there. . . . I
really do have to make it clear here that this feeling of discouragement was not at all like the misery that accompanied
the "personal" scenes; no, even at the worst, the disorder and
anarchy of the rooms were nothing like as bad as the shut-in
stuffiness of the family, the "personal"; it was always a liberation to step away from my "real" life into this other place, so
full of possibilities, of alternatives. When I talk of "lowering"
here, I mean only in terms of the generally freer air of this
region; I could not compare it with the constrictions and con-
finements of the place, or the time, where that family lived out
its little puppet play.

But what laws, or needs, did the unknown destroyer obey?
I would find myself in the long but irregular passage—like
a wide hallway that extended itself indefinitely, full of doors
and little enclaves where a table might stand with flowers or a
statue, pictures, objects of all kinds, each with an exact place
—and open a door on a room next to it and there everything
would be awry. A violent wind would be blowing the curtains
straight out into the room, knocking over small tables, sweeping books off the arms of chairs, littering the carpet with ash
and cigarette stubs from an ashtray which was wheeling there,
ready to topple. Opening another door, I found that everything
stood as it ought: there was order, a room not only ready for
its occupants, as neat as a hotel bedroom, but one which he,
she, they, had just left, for I could feel a personality or presences
in a room seen through a half-open door. Which, entering,
perhaps only a moment later, I might find in chaos, as if it
were a room in a doll's house, and the hand of the little girl
had been inserted through the ceiling and knocked everything
over on a freak of impulse or bad temper.

I decided that what I had to do was repaint the rooms.
. . . I talk as if they were a permanent, recognisable, stable set
of rooms, as in a house or a flat, instead of a place which
changed each time I saw it. First, paint: what was the use of
tidying or cleaning furniture that would have to stand between
such forlorn and shabby walls? I found paints. Tins of different sizes and colours stood waiting on spread newspapers on
the floor in one of the rooms that was temporarily empty—I
had seen it furnished only a few minutes before. There were
brushes and bottles of turpentine and the painter's ladder I
had seen during one of my early visits here. I started on a room
I knew well: it was the drawing-room that had brocade curtains and pink and green silks and old wood. I stacked what
was usable in the middle of the room under dust-sheets. I
scrubbed down the ceiling and walls with sugar soap, with hot
water, with detergents. Layer after layer of white paint went
on, first dull and flat, then increasingly fine, until the last one
covered everything with a clear softly shining enamel, white
as new snow or fine china. It was like standing inside a
cleaned-out eggshell; I felt that accretions of grime had been
taken off which had been preventing a living thing from
breathing. I left the furniture there in the centre of the room
under its shrouds, for it seemed too shabby now for such a
fine room, and I felt that there seemed little point in setting
it out: when I returned the poltergeist would have flung everything about or thrown muck at the walls. But no, it was not
so; this did not happen, or I think it did not—for I never saw
that room again. And it was not that I looked for it and failed
to find it. . . . Would it be accurate to say that I forgot it? That
would be to talk of that place in terms of our ordinary living.
While I was in that room, the task made sense; there was
continuity to what I did, a future, and I was in a continuing
relation to the invisible destructive creature, or force, just as I

was with the other beneficent presence. But this feeling of
relatedness, of connection, of context, belonged to that particular visit to the room, and on the next visit it was not the
same room, and my preoccupation with it was altered—and so
with the other rooms, other scenes, whose flavours and scents
held total authenticity for the time they lasted and not a moment longer.

I have been writing, with no particular reluctance or lack
of enjoyment, descriptions of the realm of anarchy, of change,
of impermanence; now I must return to the "personal" and it
is with dismay, a not-wanting. . . .

I had approached a door, apprehensive but also curious to
see if I would open it on the poltergeist's work, but instead it
was a scene of clean tidiness, a room that oppressed and dis-
couraged because of its statement that here everything had its
place and its time, that nothing could change or move out of
its order.

The walls were ruthless; the furniture heavy, polished,
shining; sofas and chairs were like large people making conversation; the legs of a great table bruised the carpet.

There were people. Real people, not forces or presences.
Dominant among them was a woman, one I had seen before,
knew well. She was tall, large, with a clean-china healthiness,
all blue eyes, pink cheeks, and the jolly no-nonsense mouth of a
schoolgirl. Her hair was brown, and there was a great deal of
it piled on the top of her head and firmly held there. She was
dressed for company; she wore good clothes, expensive,
fashionable, and inside them her body seemed to be trying to
assert itself—timidly, but with a certain courage, even gallantry.
Her arms and legs looked uncomfortable; she had not wanted
to put on these clothes, but had felt she must; she would discard them with a small laugh, a sigh, and "Thank the Lord
for that; what a relief!"

She was talking to a woman, the visitor, whose back was to me. I could watch her face, her eyes. Those eyes, unclouded by self-criticism, like skies that have been blue for too many weeks, and will continue blue and regular for weeks yet, for it is nowhere near the time for the season to change—her eyes were blank, did not see the woman she was talking to, nor the small child in her lap, whom she bumped up and down energetically, using her heel as a spring. Nor did she see the little girl who stood a short way from her mother, watching, listening, all her senses stretched, as if every pore took in information in the form of warnings, threats, messages of dislike. From this child emanated strong waves of painful emotion. It was guilt. She was condemned. And as I recognised this emotion and the group of people there in the heavy comfortable room, the scene formalised itself like a Victorian problem picture or a photograph from an old-fashioned play. Over it was written in emphatic script: "*GUILT.*"

In the background was a man, looking uncomfortable. He was a soldier, or had been one. He was tall, and built well, but held himself as if it were hard to maintain purpose and self-respect. His conventionally handsome face was sensitive and easily pained, and was half-hidden by a large moustache.

The woman, the wife and mother, was talking; she talked, she talked, she went on and on as if no one but herself existed in that room or beyond it, as if she were alone and her husband and her children—the little girl particularly, who knew she was the chief culprit, the one being complained of—couldn't hear her.

"But I simply did not expect it, no one ever warns one how it is going to be, it is too much. By the time the end of the day has come, I'm not fit for anything at all but sleep, my mind is just a fog, it's a scramble. . . . As for reading or any serious sort of thing, that is out of the question. Emily will wake at six, I've trained her to stay quiet until seven, but from then on, I'm on the go, the go, the go, all day, it is one thing after another, and when you think that at one time I was quite known for my intelligence—well, that is just a joke, I'm afraid."

The man, very still, sat back in his chair, smoking. The ash on his cigarette lengthened itself and dropped. He frowned, gave his wife an irritated look, hastily pulled an ashtray towards him in a way that said at the same time he should have remembered the ashtray before but that if he felt like dropping ash he was entitled to. He went on smoking. The little girl, who was about five or six, had her thumb in her mouth. Her face was shadowed and bleak because of the pressure of criticism on her, her existence.

She was a dark-haired child, with dark eyes like her father's, full of pain—guilt.

"No one has any idea, do they, until they have children, what it means. It's all I can do just to keep up with the rush of things, the meals one after another, the food, let alone giving the children the attention they should have. I know that Emily is ready for more than I have time to give her, but she is such a demanding child, so difficult, she always has taken a lot out of me, she wants to be read to and played with all the time, but I'm cooking, I'm ordering food, I'm at it all day— well, you know how it is, there isn't time for what has to be done, I simply don't have time for the child. I did manage to get a girl for a time last year, but that was really more trouble than it was worth, really, all their problems and their crises and you have to deal with them, she took up as much of my time as Emily does, but I did get an hour to myself after lunch and I put my feet up for a bit, but I did not find I had the energy to read, let alone study, no one knows how it is, what it means, no, children do for you, they do you in, I'm not what I was—I know that only too well, I am afraid."

The child on her knee, two or three years old, a heavy passive child dressed in white wool that smelled damp, was being jogged faster now; his eyes were glazing as the world bounced up and down around him, his adenoidal mouth was open and slack, the full cheeks quivering.

The husband, passive but really tense with irritation—with guilt—smoked on, listening, frowning.

"But what can you give out when you get nothing in? I am empty, drained; I am exhausted by lunchtime and all I want is to sleep by then. And when you think of what I used to be, what I was capable of! I never thought of being tired. I never imagined I could become the sort of woman who would never have time to open a book. But there it is."

She sighed, quite unselfconsciously. She was like a child, that tall, solid, confident woman; she needed understanding as a child does. She sat looking inward into the demands of her days and her nights. No one else was there, for her, because she felt she was talking to herself: they could not hear, or would not. She was trapped, but did not know why she felt this, for her marriage and her children were what she personally had wanted and had aimed for—what society had chosen for her. Nothing in her education or experience had prepared her for what she did in fact feel, and she was isolated in her distress and her bafflement, sometimes even believing that she might perhaps be ill in some way.

The little girl, Emily, had left the chair where she had been standing and holding tight to the arm, sheltering from the storm of abuse and criticism. She now went to her father and stood by his knee, watching that great powerful woman, her mother, whose hands were so strong and so hurtful. She was shrinking closer and closer to her father, who, it seemed, was unaware of her. He made a clumsy movement, knocking off his ashtray, and his instinctive retrieval of it caused his elbow to jog Emily. She fell back, dropped away, like something left behind as a rush of water goes past, or a stream of air. She drifted to the floor and lay there, face downwards, thumb in her mouth.

The hard accusing voice went on and on, would always go on, had always gone on; nothing could stop it, could end these emotions, this pain, this guilt at ever having been born at all, born to cause such pain and annoyance and difficulty. The voice would nag on there forever, could never be turned off, and even when the sound was turned low in memory, there must be a permanent pressure of dislike, resentment. Often in my ordinary life I would hear the sound of a voice, a bitter and low complaint just the other side of sense: there it was, in one of the rooms behind the wall, still there, always there. . . . Standing at the window, I watched Emily, the bright attractive girl who always had people around her listening to her chatter, her laugh, her little clevernesses. She was always aware of everything that went on; nothing could escape her in the movements and happenings of that crowd; while talking with one group, it seemed as if even her back and shoulders were taking in information from another. And yet she was isolated, alone; the "attractiveness" was like a shell of bright paint, and from inside it she watched and listened. It was the intensity of her self-awareness that made her alone; this did not leave her, even at her most feverish, when she was tipsy or drunk, or singing with the others. It was as if she had an invisible deformity, a hump on her back, perhaps, visible only to herself . . . and to me, as I stood watching her in a way I never could when she was close to me at home.

Emily might not see me at all. So much aware of what went on among her companions, she had eyes for very little outside. But she did notice me once or twice, and then it was odd to see how she would look at me, just as if I could not see her looking. It was as if the act of her gazing out from the protection of that crowd gave her immunity, was a different thing from looking at someone inside it, demanding a different code. A long, level thoughtful stare, not unfriendly, merely detached: something would remind her that she was totally exposed, her real self visible, and then would come the bright hard smile, the wave of the hand—friendliness, as far as it was licensed by her companions. As soon as she lost sight of me, my existence vanished for her; she was back again, enclosed by them, the prisoner of her situation.

While I stood by the window, Hugo watchful beside me, observing her, I saw how the numbers on the pavement had grown: fifty or more of them now, and, looking up at the innumerable windows full of faces that overhung the scene, I knew that we all had one thing in common: we were wondering how soon this throng, or part of it, would move on and away, how soon "the youngsters" would be off. . . . It would not be long now. And Emily? She would go with them? I stood by the watching yellow beast who would never let me fondle him, but who seemed to like my being there, close, the friend of his mistress, his love—I stood there and thought that any day I could approach that window and find the opposite pavement empty, the street cleaners swilling water and disinfectant, clearing away all memories of the tribe. And Hugo and I would be alone, and I would have betrayed my trust.

She did sit with her yellow animal in the mornings; she fed him his meat substitutes and his vegetables; she fondled him and talked to him; she took him at night into her little room where he lay by her bed as she slept. She loved him—

there was no doubt of that—as much as ever she had done. But she was not able to include him in her real life on the pavement.

One early evening, she came in at the time when the life outside was at its most lively, its noisiest—that is, just as the lights were beginning to appear at their different heights in the darkening air. She came in, and with a look of trepidation which she was trying to hide from me, she said to Hugo, "Come on, come with me and be introduced."

She had forgotten her earlier experiment? No, of course not; but it seemed to her that things could have changed. She was now well-known out there—more, she must feel herself to be a founder-member of this particular tribe: she had helped to form it.

He did not want to go. Oh, no, he very much did not want to go with her. He was laying the responsibility for what might happen on her in the way he stood up, signifying his willingness, or at least his agreement, to go with her.

She led the way out, and he followed. She had not put him on his heavy chain. She was, in leaving her animal unprotected, making her pack responsible for their behaviour.

I watched the young girl—slender and vulnerable even in her thick trousers, her boots, her jacket, her scarves—cross the road, with her beast following soberly after her. She was afraid, that was obvious, as she stood on the edge of one of the bright chattering noisy groups which always seemed lit with an inner violence of excitement or of readiness for excitement. She kept her hand down on the beast's head, for reassurance. People turned and saw her, saw Hugo. Both the girl and the animal had their backs to me; I was able to see the throng of faces as Emily and Hugo saw them. I did not like what I saw. . . . If I had been out there I would have wanted to run, to get away. . . . But she stuck it out for a time. Her hand always kept down, close to Hugo's head, fondling his ears, patting him, soothing, she moved quietly among the clans, determined to make her test, to sound out her position with them. She stayed out with him as dusk came down and the lively crowds were absorbed into a mingle of light and dark, where sound—a laugh, a raised voice, the clink of a bottle—was heightened, and went travelling out in every direction to the now invisible watchers at their windows, carrying messages of excitement or alarm.

When she brought him in, she seemed tired. She was saddened. She was much closer to the commonplace level where I, as one of the elderly, lived. Her eyes saw me as she sat eating her bean salad, her little hunk of bread; seemed really to see the room we sat in. As for me, I was full of apprehension; I believed her sadness was because she had decided her Hugo could not safely travel with the tribe—I thought her mad even to have considered it—and that she had decided to leave with them, to jettison him.

After the meal, she sat for a long time at the window. She gazed at the scene she was usually a part of. The animal sat not beside her but quietly in a corner. You could believe he was weeping, or would if he knew how. He sorrowed inwardly. His lids lowered themselves as crises of pain gripped him, and he would give a great shiver.

When Emily went to bed, she had to call him several times, and he went at last, slowly, with a quiet dignified padding. But he was in inner isolation from her: he was protecting himself.

Next morning she offered to go out and forage for supplies. She had not done this for some time, and again I felt this was some sort of token apology because she meant to leave.

We two sat on quietly in the long room, which the sunlight had left because it was already midday. I was at one side
of it, and Hugo lay stretched, head on paws, along the outer
wall of the room where he could not be seen from the windows
above him.

We heard footsteps outside which stopped, then became
stealthy. We heard voices that had been loud, suddenly soft.

A young girl's voice? No, a boy's; but it was hard to tell.
Two heads appeared at the window, trying to see in the com-
parative dusk of the room: the light was brilliant outside.

"It's here," said one of the Mehta boys, from upstairs.

"I've seen him at the window," said a black youth. I had
observed him often with the others on the pavement, a slim,
lithe, likeable boy. A third head appeared between the other
two: a white girl, from one of the blocks of flats.

"Stewed dog," she said daintily. "Well, *I'm* not going to
eat it."

"Oh, go on," said the black boy, "I've seen what you eat."

I heard a rattling sound; it was Hugo. He was trembling,
and his claws were rattling on the floorboards.

Then the girl saw me sitting there, recognised me, and put
on the bright uncaring grin the pack allowed outsiders.

"Oh," she said, "we thought . . ."

"No," I said. "I'm living here. I haven't left."

The three faces briefly turned towards each other, brown,
white, black, as they put on for each other's benefit *We've
made a mess of it* grimaces. They faded outwards, leaving the
window empty.

There was a soft moaning from Hugo.

"It's all right," I said. "They've gone."

The rattling sound increased. Then the animal heaved
himself up and crept away, with an attempt at dignity, towards

the door into the open kitchen, which was the farthest he could go from the dangerous window. He did not want me to observe his loss of self-possession. He was ashamed of having lost it. The moaning I had heard was as much shame as because he was afraid.

When Emily came in, a good girl, daughter of the house, it was evening. She was tired, had had to visit many places to find supplies. But she was pleased with herself. The rations at that time were minimal, because of the winter just finished: swedes, potatoes, cabbage, onions. That was about it. But she had managed to find a few eggs, a little fish, and even—a prize—a strongly scented, unshrivelled lemon. I told her, when she had finished showing off her booty, what had happened. At once her good spirits went. She sat quiet, head lowered, eyes concealed from me by the thick, white, heavily lashed lids. Then, without looking at me, turning herself from me, she went to find her Hugo, to comfort him.

And then, a little later, out she went to the pavement and stayed there until very late.

I remember how I sat on and on in the dark. I was putting off the moment of lighting the candles, thinking that the soft square of light, which was how my window looked from across the street, would remind the cannibals out there of Hugo. Who was back in the place along the wall where he could not easily be seen. He was as still as if asleep, but his eyes were open. When I did light the candles, he did not move or even blink.

Looking back, I see myself sitting in the long room with its comfortable old furniture, with Emily's things in the little space she allotted for them, and the yellow beast lying quietly, suffering. And there for backdrop was the ambiguous wall, which could so easily dissolve, dissolving, too, all this ex-

traneous life, and the anxieties and pressures of the time—
creating, of course, its own. Shadowily present, there it stood,
its pattern of fruits and leaves and flowers obliterated by the
dim light. That is how I see it, see us: the long room, dimly
lit, with me and Hugo there, thinking of Emily away across
the street among crowds that shifted and ebbed and thinned
and left—and behind us that other indefinite region, shifting
and melting and changing, where walls and doors and rooms
and gardens and people continually re-created themselves, like
clouds.

That night there was a moon. There seemed more light
outside my room than in it. The pavements were crammed.
There was a lot of noise.

It was clear that the crowd had split into two parts: one
part was about to take to the roads.

I looked for Emily with these people, but could not see
her. Then I did see her: she was with the people who were
staying behind. We all—I, Hugo, the part of the crowd not
yet ready to make the journey, and the hundreds of people
at the windows all around and above—watched as the departing ones formed up into a regiment, four or five abreast. They
did not seem to be taking much with them, but summer lay
ahead, and the country they were heading for was still—or
so we believed—not yet much pillaged. They were mostly very
young, people not yet twenty, but included a family of mother
and father with three small children. A baby was carried in
the arms of a friend, the mother took an infant on her back
in a sling, the father had the biggest child on his shoulders.
There were leaders, three men: not the middle-aged or older
men, but the older ones among the young people. Of these,
two went at the front with their women, and one came at the
end with his: he had two girls attached to him. There were
about forty people altogether in this band.

They had a cart or trolley, similar to the ones that had been used at airports and railway stations. This had some parcels of root vegetables and grain on it, and the little bundles of the travellers. Also, at the last moment, a couple of youths, laughing but still shamefaced, or at least self-conscious, pushed on to this trolley a great limp parcel which exuded blood.

There were slim bundles of reeds on the cart—these were hawked from door to door by then—and three girls carried them as flaring torches, one at the front, one at the back, one in the middle, torches much brighter than the street lighting, which was inadequate when it was not altogether absent. And off they went, along the road north-west, lit by the torches that dripped dangerous fire close above their heads. They were singing. They sang "Show Me the Way to Go Home"—without, or so it seemed, any consciousness of its ludicrous pathos. They sang "We Shall Not Be Moved," and "Down by the Riverside."

They had gone, and left on the pavements were still a good many people. These seemed subdued, and soon dispersed. Emily came in, silent. She looked for Hugo; he had returned to his place along the wall, and she sat near him and pulled his front half over her lap. She sat there hugging him, bent over him. I could see the big yellow head lying on her arm, could hear him, at last, purr and croon.

Now I knew that while she wanted more than anything to be off into that savage gamblers' future with the migrating ones, she was not prepared to sacrifice her Hugo. Or, at least, was in conflict. And I dared to hope. Yet, even while I did, I wondered why I thought it mattered that she should stay. Stay with what? Me? Did I believe it mattered that she should stay where she had been left by that man? Well, my faith in that was beginning to dim; but her survival mattered, presumably, and who could say where she was likely to be safest? Did I believe that she should stay with her animal? Yes, I did; absurdly, of course, for he was only a beast. But he was hers, she loved him, she must care for him; she could not leave him without harm to herself. So I told myself, argued with myself, comforted myself—argued, too, with that invisible mentor, the man who had dropped Emily with me and gone off: how was I to know what to do? Or how to think? If I was making mistakes, then whose fault was it? He had not told me anything, or left instructions; there was no way at all of my knowing how I was expected to be living, how Emily should be living.

Behind the wall I found a room that was tall, not very large, and I think six-sided. There was no furniture in it, only a rough trestle around two of the sides. On the floor was spread a carpet, but it was a carpet without its life: it had a design, an intricate one, but the colours had an imminent existence, a potential, no more. There had been a fair or a market here, and this had left a quantity of rags, dress materials, scraps of Eastern embroideries of the kind that have tiny mirrors buttonhole-stitched into them, old clothes—everything in that line you can think of. Some people were standing about the room. At first it seemed that they were doing nothing at all; they looked idle and undecided. Then one of them detached a piece of material from the jumble on the trestles, and bent to match it with the carpet—behold, the pattern answered that part of the carpet. This piece was laid exactly on the design, and brought it to life.

It was like a child's game, giant-sized; only it was not a game; it was serious, important not only to the people actually engaged in this work, but to everyone. Then another person bent with a piece chosen from the multicoloured heap on the trestles, bent, matched, and straightened again to gaze down.

There they stood, about a dozen people, quite silent, turning their eyes from the patterns of the carpet to the tangle of stuffs and back again. A recognition, the quick move, a smile of pleasure or of relief, a congratulatory glance from one of the others—there was no competition here, only the soberest and most loving co-operation. I entered the room; I stood on the carpet looking down as they did at its incompleteness, pattern without colour, except where the pieces had already been laid in a match, so that parts of the carpet had a bleak gleam, like one that has been bleached, and other parts glowed up, fulfilled, perfect. I, too, sought for fragments of materials that could bring life to the carpet, and did in fact find one, and bent down to match and fit, before some pressure moved me on again. I realised that everywhere around, in all the other rooms, were people who would in their turn drift in here, see this central activity, find their matching piece—would lay it down, and drift off again to other tasks. I left that tall room whose ceiling vanished upwards into dark where I thought I saw the shine of a star, a room whose lower part was in a bright light that enclosed the silent concentrated figures like stage-lighting. I left them and moved on. The room disappeared. I could not find it when I turned my head to see it again, so as to mark where it was. But I knew it was there waiting; I knew it had not disappeared, and the work in it continued, must continue, would go on always.

□   □   □

This time seems now to have gone on and on, yet in fact it was quite short, a matter of months. So much was happening, and every hour seemed crammed with new experience. Yet in appearance all I did was to live quietly there, in that room, with Hugo, with Emily. Inside it was all chaos: the feeling one is taken over by, at the times in one's life when everything is in change, movement, destruction—or reconstruction, but that is not always evident at the time—a feeling of helplessness, as if one were being whirled about in a dustdevil or a centrifuge.

Yet I had no alternative but to go on doing exactly what I was. Watching and waiting. Watching, for the most part, Emily . . . who had been a stranger, so it seemed, for years. But of course this was not so; it was anxiety for her that stretched the hours. The yellow beast, melancholy, his sorrow swallowed—I swear this was so, though he was no more than animal—in the determination to be stoic, not to show his wounds, sat quietly at the window in a place behind the curtains, where he could easily dodge back and down, or stretched along the wall in a mourner's position, his head on his forepaws, his green eyes steady and open. He lay there hour after hour, contemplating his—thoughts. Why not? He thought, he judged, as animals can be seen to do, if observed without prejudice. I must say here, since it has to be said somewhere about Hugo, that I think the series of comments automatically evoked by this kind of statement, the ticker-tape remarks to do with "anthropomorphism," are beside the point. Our emotional life is shared with the animals; we flatter ourselves that human emotions are so much more complicated than theirs. Perhaps the only emotion not known to a cat or a dog is—romantic love. And even then we have to wonder. What is the emotional devotion of a dog for his master or mistress but something like that sort of love, all pining and yearning and "give me, give me." What was Hugo's love for Emily but that? As for our thoughts, our intellectual apparatus, our rationalisms and our logics and our deductions, and so on, it can be said with absolute certainty that dogs and cats and monkeys cannot make a rocket to fly to the moon or weave artificial dress materials out of the by-products of petroleum, but as we sit in the ruins of this variety of intelligence, it is hard to give it much value: I suppose we are under-valuing it now as we over-valued it then. It will have to find its place: I believe a pretty low place, at that.

I think that all this time human beings have been watched by creatures whose perceptions and understanding have been so far in advance of anything we have been able to accept, because of our vanity, that we would be appalled if we were able to know, would be humiliated. We have been living with them as blundering, blind, callous, cruel murderers and torturers, and they have watched and known us. And this is the reason we refuse to acknowledge the intelligence of the creatures that surround us: the shock to our *amour-propre* would be too much, the judgement we would have to make on ourselves too horrible. It is exactly the same process that can make someone go on and on committing a crime, or a cruelty, knowing it: the stopping and having to see what has been done would be too painful; one cannot face it.

But people need slaves and victims and appendages, and of course many of our "pets" are that, because they have been made into what we think they should be, just as human beings can become what they are expected to be. But not all, not by any means; all the time, through our lives, we are accompanied, everywhere we go, by creatures who judge us, and who behave at times with a nobility which is . . . we call it human.

Hugo, this botch of a creature, was in his relations with Emily as delicate as a faithful lover who is content with very little provided he is not banished from the beloved presence. This is what he had imposed on himself: he would not make demands, not ask, not be a nuisance. He was waiting. As I was. He watched, as I did.

I was spending long hours with him. Or I sat at the times when the sunlight was on the wall, waiting for it to open, to unfold. Or I went about the streets, taking in news and rumours and information with the rest, wondering what to do for the best, and deciding to do nothing for the time being; wondering how long this city would stand, eroded as it was in every way, its services going and gone, its people fleeing, its food supplies worsening, its law and order consisting more and more of what the citizens imposed on themselves, an instinctive self-restraint, even a caring for others who were in the same straits.

There seemed to be a new sharpness in the tension of waiting. For one thing, the weather—the summer had come hot and dry, the sun had a dusty look. The pavement opposite my window had filled up again. But there was less interest now in what went on out there: the windows held fewer heads, people had become used to it all. Everyone knew that again and again the street's edge would half empty as another tribe took off, and we acknowledged with mixed feelings the chance that had chosen our street as a gathering place for the migrations from our part of the city: parents at least knew what their children were doing, even if they did not like it. We became accustomed to watching a mixed lot of people collect along the pavement with their pathetic bits of baggage, and then depart, singing their old wartime songs, or revolutionary songs that seemed as inappropriate as sex songs are to old age. And Emily did not leave. She would run after them a little way with some of the other girls, and then come home, subdued, to put her arms around her Hugo, her dark head down on his yellow coat. It was as if they both wept. They huddled together, creatures in sorrow, comforting each other.

The next thing was that Emily fell in love. . . . I am conscious that this seems a term inappropriate to the times I am describing. It was with a young man who seemed likely to lead the next contingent out and away from the city. He was, despite his swashbuckling clothes, a thoughtful young man, or at least one slow to judgement; an observer by temperament, perhaps, but pushed into action by the time? He was, at any rate, the natural guardian of the younger ones, the distressed, the forlorn. He was known for this, teased for it, sometimes criticised: softness of this sort was superfluous to the demands of survival. Perhaps this was why he appealed to Emily.

I believe her trust in him was such that she even thought of taking Hugo out to the mob for another trial, but this must have gone from her to Hugo, for he felt it: he shivered and shrank, and she had to put her arms around him and say, "No, I won't, Hugo; I promise I won't. Did you hear? I promised, didn't I?"

Well, then, so there it was: she was infatuated. It was "the first love" of tradition. Which is to say that half a dozen puppy loves, each one as agonising and every bit as intense and serious as later "adult" loves, had passed; this love was "first" and "serious" because it was returned, or at least acknowledged.

I remember I used to wonder if these young people, living as they had to from hand to mouth, who would never shut themselves off in couples behind walls unless it was for a few days or hours in a deserted house somewhere, or a shed in a field, would ever say to each other, "I love you." "Do you love me?" "Will our love last?"—and so on. All of which phrases seemed more and more like the keys or documents of possession to states and conditions now obsolete.

But Emily was suffering, she was in pain, as one is at that age, as fresh as a new loaf, and loving a hero of twenty-two. Who had inexplicably, even eerily, chosen her. She was his girl chosen from many, and known as such. She was beside him on the pavement, went with him on expeditions, and people felt pleasure and even importance when they called to her: "Gerald says . . ." "Gerald wants you to . . ."

From pain she would soar at once to exaltation, and stood there beside him, flushed and beautiful, her eyes soft. Or fling herself down in the sofa corner, to be by herself for a bit, or at least away from him, for it was all too much, too powerful; she needed a respite. She was radiant with amazement, not seeing me or her surroundings, and I knew she was saying to herself, "But he's chosen *me, me*" . . . and this did not mean *And I'm only thirteen!* That was a thought for people my age. A girl was ready for mating when her body was.

But these young people's lives were communal, and mating was far from being the focus or pivot of a relationship when they chose each other. No, any individual consummations were nothing beside this act of mingling constantly with others, as if some giant rite of eating were taking place, everyone tasting and licking and regurgitating everyone else, making themselves known to others and others known to them in this tasting and sampling—eyeing each other, rubbing shoulders and bodies, talking, exchanging emanations.

But while Emily was part of this communal act, the communal feast, she was at the same time feeling as girls traditionally did. She wanted, I knew, to be alone with Gerald: she would have liked that experience, the old one.

But she never was alone with him.

What she wanted was inappropriate. She felt in the wrong, even criminal—at least very much to be blamed. She was an anachronism.

I did not say anything, for our relations were not such that I could ask, or she likely to volunteer.

All I knew was what I could see for myself: that she was being filled over and over again with a violence of need that exploded in her, dazzling her eyes and shaking her body so that she was astonished—needs which could never be slaked by an embrace on the floorboards of an empty room or in the corner of a field. All around her the business of living went on, but Gerald was always at the heart of it: wherever she turned herself in some task or duty, there he was, so efficient and practical and busy with important things, but she, Emily, was possessed by a savage enemy, was raging with joy and grief. And if she betrayed what she felt by a wrong look or a word, what then? She would lose her home here, among these people, *her* tribe. . . . And this was why she had so often to slip away indoors, to creep near her familiar Hugo, and put her arms around him. At which he might give a muffled groan, since he knew very well the use she was making of him.

There was this juxtaposition: Emily lay with her cheek on rough yellow fur, one still-childish hand enclosing a ragged ear, her tense body expressing emptiness and longing. The wall beside me opened, reminding me again how easily and unexpectedly it could, and I was walking towards a door from which voices came. And frenetic laughter, squeals, protests. I opened the door on that world whose air was irritation, confinement, littleness. A brightly coloured world: the colours were flat and loud as in old calendars. A hot close place, everything very large, over-lifesize, difficult: this was again the child's view that I was imprisoned in. Largeness and smallness; violence of emotion and its insignificance—contradictions, impossibilities were built into and formed part of the substance of whatever one saw when that particular climate was entered. It was a bedroom. Again a fire burned in the wall behind a tall metal guard. Again it was a thick, heavy, absorbing room, with time as its air, the tick of a clock felt as a condition of one's every moment and thought. The room was full of a hot light: a reddish light barred and crossed with shadow lay over the walls, across the ceiling, and on the immensely long soft white curtains that filled a wall opposite the two beds: father's and mother's beds, husband's bed and wife's bed.

The curtains for some reason filled me with anguish, the soft weight of them. They were of white lawn or muslin that had a raised spot woven in, and were lined and lined again. A white that was made for lightness and transparency to let in sun and night-air had been taken hold of and thickened and made heavy and hung up in shrouds to shut out air and light, to reflect hot flame-light from the metal-barred fireplace.

On one side of the room the mother sat with her boy-infant, always in his damp wool. Her arms were about him, she was absorbed in him. In a large chair set against the curtains, the soldier-like man sat with his knees apart, gripping between them the small girl who stood shrieking. On his face, under the moustache, was a small tight smile. He was "tickling" the child. This was a "game," the bedtime "game," a ritual. The elder child was being played with, was being made tired, was being given her allowance of attention, before being put to bed, and it was a service by the father to the mother, who could not cope with the demands of her day, the demands of Emily. The child wore a long nightie, with frills at wrists and at the neck. Her hair had been brushed and was held by ribbon. A few minutes ago she had been a clean neat pretty little girl in a white nightdress, with a white ribbon in her hair, but now she was hot and sweating, and her body was contorting and twisting to escape the man's great hands that squeezed and dug into her ribs, to escape the great cruel face that bent so close over her with its look of private satisfaction. The room seemed filled with a hot anguish, the fear of being held tight there, the need for being held and tortured, since this was how she pleased her captors. She shrieked: "No, no, no, no" . . . helpless, being explored and laid bare by this man.

The mother was indifferent. She did not know what was going on, or what the little girl suffered. For it was a "game," and the squeals and protests were from her own childhood, and therefore in order, healthy, licensed. From her came a blankness, the indifference of ignorance. She cooed and talked to her stolid open-mouthed infant while the father went on with his task, from time to time looking at his wife with a wonderfully complex expression—guilt, but he was unaware of that; appeal, because he felt this was wrong and ought to be stopped; astonishment that it was allowable and by her, who not only did not protest, but actively encouraged him in the "game"; and, mingled with all these, a look that was never far from his face at any time of sheer incredulity at the impossibility of everything. He let his knees go slack and pretended to release the child, who nearly fell, reached for a knee to steady herself, but before she could run away, was caught again as the knees clapped together on either side of her. The exquisite torture began again. "There, there, there, Emily," muttered the great man, flooding her in an odour of tobacco and unwashed clothes. "Now, then, that's it; there you are, you see," he went on as the fingers, thicker than any of her ribs, dug into her sides and she screamed and pleaded.

This scene faded like a spark or like a nightmare, and the same man was sitting in the same room but in a chair near the bed. He wore a heavy brown dressing gown of some very thick rough wool, a soldier's garment, and he smoked and sat watching his wife. The large healthy woman was discarding her clothes in a rapid efficient way on her side of the bed near the fire: only now it was summer, and the fireplace had red flowers standing in it. The curtains hung limp and still, very white, but drawn back to show areas of black glass, which reflected the man, the room, the movements of the woman. She was unaware of her husband, who sat watching her nakedness emerge. She was talking, she was creating her day for him, for herself: "And by four o'clock I was quite exhausted, the girl had her half-day, and Baby was awake all morning, he did not have his sleep, and Emily was very trying and demanding today ... and ... and ..." The plaint went on while she stood naked, looking about her for pyjamas. She was a fine solid woman with clear white flesh, her breasts small and round. The nipples were virginal for a woman who had had two children: small and with narrow pink aureoles. Her plentiful brown hair fell down her back, and she scratched first her scalp, then under one arm, lifting it to expose wisps of long brown hair. On to her face came a look of intense satisfaction which would have appalled her if she could have seen it. She scratched the other armpit, then allowed herself to scratch, voluptuously, with both hands, her ribs, her hips, her stomach. Her hands did not stray lower. She stood there scratching vigorously for a long time, a couple of minutes, while red marks appeared on the solid white flesh behind the energetic fingers, and from time to time she gave a great shudder of pleasure, masked as cold. Her husband sat quiet and watched. On his face was a small smile. He lifted his cigarette to his mouth and took a deep lungful, and slowly let it out, allowing it to trickle from half-open mouth and nostrils.

His wife had finished with her scratching and was bundling herself into pink-spotted cotton pyjamas, in which she looked like a jolly schoolgirl. Her face was unconsciously greedy—for sleep. She was already in imagination drifting to oblivion. She got efficiently into bed, as if her husband did not exist, and in one movement lay down and turned her back to him. She yawned. Then she remembered him: there was something she ought to do before allowing herself this supreme pleasure. She turned over and said, "Good night, old thing," and was at once sucked down and lay asleep, facing him. He sat on, smoking, now openly examining her at his leisure. The amusement was there, incredulity, and, at the same time, an austerity that had begun, from the look of it, as a variety of moral exhaustion, even a lack of vitality, and had long ago become a judgement on himself and on others.

He now put his cigarette out and got up from the chair, gently, as if afraid of waking a child. He went into the next room, which was the nursery with its red velvet curtains, its white, white, white everywhere. Two cots, one small one, one large. He walked delicately, a large man among a thousand tiny items of nursery use, past the small cot, to the large one. He stood at the foot of it and looked at the little girl, now asleep. Her cheeks flamed scarlet. Beads of sweat stood on her forehead. She was only lightly asleep. She kicked off the bedclothes as he watched, turned herself, and lay, her nightgown around her waist, showing small buttocks and the backs of pretty legs. The man bent lower and gazed, and gazed. . . . A noise from the bedroom, his wife turning over and perhaps saying something in her sleep, made him stand straight and look—guilty but defiant, and, above all, angry. Angry at what?

At everything, that is the answer. There was silence again.
Lower down in this tall house, a clock chimed: it was only
eleven. The little girl tossed herself over again and lay on her
back, naked, stomach thrust up, vulva prominent. The man's
face added another emotion to those already written there.
Suddenly—but, in spite of everything, not roughly—he pulled
a cover over the child and tucked it in tight. At once she began
to squirm and whimper. The room was much too hot. The
windows were closed. He was about to open one, but remembered a prohibition. He turned himself about and walked out
of the nursery without looking again at the two cots, where
the little boy lay silent, his mouth open, but where the girl was
tossing and struggling to get out, to get out, to get out.

In a room that had windows open to a formal garden,
a room that had a "feel" to it of another country somewhere,
different from the rooms in this house, was a small bed in
which the girl lay. She was older, and she was sick and fretful.
Paler, thinner than at any time I had seen her; her dark hair
was damp and sticky, and there was the smell of stale sweat.
All around her lay books, toys, comics. She was moving rest-
lessly and continuously, rubbing her limbs together, tossing
about, turning over, crooning to herself, muttering complaints
and commands to someone. She was an earthquake of fevers,
energies, desires, angers, need. In came the tall large woman,
preoccupied with a glass she was carrying. At the sight of the
glass, the girl brightened: here at least was a diversion, and she
half sat up. But already her mother had set down the glass and
was turning away to another duty.

"Stay with me," pleaded the girl.

"I can't, I have to see to Baby."

"Why do you always call him Baby?"

"I don't know, really; of course it is time—he's quite old
enough to—but I keep forgetting."

"Please, please."

"Oh, very well, for a minute."

The woman sat on the extreme edge of the bed, looked harried; looked, as she always did, burdened and irritated. But she was also pleased.

"Drink your lemonade."

"I don't want to. Mummy, cuddle me, cuddle me. . . ."

"Oh, Emily!"

With a flattered laugh, the woman bent forward, offering herself. The little girl put her arms up around the woman's neck and hung there. But she got no encouragement. "Cuddle me, cuddle me," she was crooning, as if to herself, and it might just as well have been to herself, since the woman was so puzzled by it all. She suffered the small hot arms for a little, but then she could not help herself—her dislike of flesh raised her own hands, to put the child's arms away from her. "There, that's enough," she said. But she stayed a little. Duty made her stay. Duty to what? Sickness, very likely. "A sick child needs its mother." Something of that sort. Between the little girl's hot needful yearning body, which wanted to be quieted with a caress, with warmth; wanted to lie near a large strong wall of a body, a safe body which would not tickle and torment and squeeze; wanted safety and assurance—between her and the mother's regularly breathing, calm body, all self-sufficiency and duty, was a blankness, an unawareness; there was no contact, no mutual comfort.

The little girl lay back and then reached for the glass and drank eagerly. The moment the glass was empty, the mother got up and said, "I'll make you another one."

"Oh, stay with me, stay with me."

"I can't, Emily. You are being difficult again."

"Can Daddy come?"

"But he's busy."

"Can't he read to me?"

"You can read to yourself now; you're a big girl."

The woman went out with the empty glass. The girl took a half-eaten biscuit from under the pillow and picked up a book and read and ate, ate and read, her limbs always on the move tossing and rearranging themselves, her unoccupied hand touching her cheek, her hair, her shoulders, feeling her flesh everywhere, lower and lower down, near to her cunt, her "private parts"—but from there the hand was quickly withdrawn, as if that area had barbed wire around it. Then she stroked her thighs, crossed and uncrossed them, moved and twisted, and read and ate and ate and read.

There lay Emily now on my living-room floor.

"Dear Hugo . . . dear, dear Hugo—you are *my* Hugo, you are my love, Hugo. . . ."

And I was filled with that ridiculous impatience, the helplessness, of the adult who watches a young thing growing. There she was, enclosed in her age, but in a continuum with those scenes behind the wall, a hinterland which had formed her—yet she could not see them or know about them, and it would be of no use my telling her: if I did, she would hear words, no more. From that shadowy region behind her came the dictate: *You are this, and this and this—this is what you have to be, and not that;* and the biological demands of her age took a precise and predictable and clock-like stake on her life, making her exactly like this and that. And so it would go on, it had to go on, and I must watch; and in due time she would fill like a container with substances and experiences; she would be delivered by these midwives, some recognisable, understood, and common to everyone, some to be deduced only from their methods of operation—she would become mature, that ideal condition envisaged as the justification of all previous experience, an apex of achievement, inevitable and peculiar to her. This apex is how we see things; it is a biological summit we see: growth, the achievement on the top of the curve of her existence as an animal, then a falling away towards death. Nonsense, of course, absurd; but it was hard to subdue in myself this view of her, to shut off impatience as I watched her rolling and snuggling beside her purring yellow beast, to make myself acknowledge that this stage of her life was every bit as valid as the one ahead of her—perhaps to be summed up or encapsulated in the image of a capable but serene smile—and that what I was really waiting for (just as, somewhere inside herself, *she* must be) was the moment she would step off this merry-go-round, this escalator carrying her from the dark into the dark. Step off it entirely. . . . And then?

☐  ☐  ☐

There was a new development in the life on the pavement. It was bound up with Gerald; with, precisely, his need to protect the weak, his identification with them, that quality which could not be included in the little balance sheets of survival. There were suddenly children out there—nine, ten, eleven years old—not attached to families, but by themselves. Some had parents they had run away from, or whom they did see, but only occasionally. Some had no parents at all. What had happened to them? It was hard to say. Officially of course children still had parents and homes and that kind of thing, and if not, they had to be in care or custody; officially children even went to school regularly. But nothing like this was the practice. Sometimes children attached themselves to other families, their own parents being unable to cope with the pressures

—not knowing where to find food and supplies, or simply losing interest and throwing them out to fend for themselves, as people had once done with dogs and cats that no longer gave pleasure. Some parents were dead, because of violence or epidemics. Others had gone away out of the city and left their children behind. These waifs tended to be ignored by the authorities unless attention was specifically drawn to them. They were still part of society, wished to be part, and hung around where people lived. They were quite unlike those children whom I will have to describe quite soon, who had put themselves outside society altogether, were our enemies.

Gerald noticed that a dozen or so children were literally living on the pavement, and began to look after them in an organised way. Emily of course adored him for this, and defended him against the inevitable criticism. It was mostly of old people that it was said they should be allowed to die—I can tell you that this added a new dimension of terror to the lives of the elderly, already tenuous—that the weaker had to go to the wall: this was already happening, and was not a process that should be checked by sickly sentiment. But Gerald took his stand. He began by defending them when people tried to chase them away. They were sleeping on the waste lot behind the pavement, and complaints started about the smell and the litter. Soon would happen what we all feared more than anything at all: the authorities would have to intervene.

There were empty houses and flats all around; about half a mile off was a large empty house, in good condition. There Gerald took the children. It had long ago lost its electricity supply, but by then hardly anyone paid for electricity. The water was still connected. The windows had been broken, but shutters were made for the ground floor and they used old bits of polythene for the upper-floor windows.

Gerald had become a father or elder brother to the children. He got food for them. Partly, he begged from shops. People were so generous. That was an odd thing: mutual aid and self-sacrifice went side by side with the callousness. And he took expeditions off to the country to get what supplies could still be bought or purloined. And, best of all, there was a large garden at the back of the house, and he taught them how to cultivate it. This was guarded day and night by the older children armed with guns or sticks, or bows and arrows or catapults.

There it was: warmth, caring, a family.

Emily believed herself to have acquired a ready-made family.

Now began a new, queer time. She was living with me, "in my care"—a joke, that, but it was still the reason for our being together. She was certainly living with her Hugo, whom she could not bear to leave. But every evening, after an early supper (and I even arranged for this meal to be at a time which would more easily accommodate her new life), she would say, "I think I'll be off now, if you don't mind." And without waiting for an answer, but giving me a small, guilty, even amused smile, she went, having kissed Hugo in a little private ceremony that was like a pact or promise. She came back, usually, at mid-morning.

I was worried of course, about pregnancy; but the conventions of our association made it impossible to ask questions, and in any case I suspected that what I regarded as an impossible burden that could drag her down, destroy her, would be greeted by her with "Well, what of it? Other people have had babies and managed, haven't they?" I was worried, too, that her attachment to this new family would become so strong that she would simply wander off, away from us, from Hugo

and me. There *we* were, the two of us, waiting. Waiting was
our occupation. We kept each other company. But he was not
mine, not my animal—most definitely he was not that. He
waited, listening, for Emily: his green eyes steady and watchful. He was always ready to get up and meet her at the door—
I knew she was coming minutes before she appeared, for he
smelled or heard or intuited her presence when she was still
streets away. At the door, the two pairs of eyes, the green,
the brown, engaged in a dazzling beam of emotion. Then she
embraced him, fed him, and bathed. There were no baths or
showers in Gerald's community yet. She dressed herself and at
once went out to the pavement.

This period, too, seemed to go on continually. That summer was a long one, the weather the same day after day. It was
hot, stuffy, noisy, dusty. Emily, like the other girls, had reverted
with the hot weather to earlier styles of dress, shedding the
thick garments that had to be worn for utility. She pulled out
the old sewing machine again and made herself some bright
fanciful dresses out of old clothes from the stalls, or she wore
the old dresses themselves. Very strange those pavements looked
to someone my age, with decades of different fashions on display there all at the same time, obliterating that sequence of
memory, that goes: "That was the year when we wore . . ."

Every day, from early afternoon onwards, Gerald, with
the children from the community house, would be on the
pavement, so Emily was separated from her "family" only for
a couple of hours each day when she paid her visit home to
dress and bath, and for an hour or so each evening when she
took a meal with me. Or, rather, with Hugo. I think, too, that
coming home for this brief time was a necessity to her emo-
tionally: she needed a respite from her emotions, her happiness. In that other house it was all a great crescendo of joy, of

success, of fulfilment, of doing, of making, of being needed. She would return from it like someone running in laughing from a heavy storm, or from too loud band music. She would alight on my sofa smiling, poised ready for flight, basking, friendly to the whole world. She could not prevent herself smiling all the time, wherever she was, so that people kept looking at her, then came to talk to her, touch her, share in the vitality that flowed off her, making a pool or reservoir of life. And in that radiant face we could still see the incredulous *But why me? This is happening to me!*

Well, and of course such intensity could not last. At its peak it was already threatened: she kept collapsing into little depressions and fatigues and irritations when the elation of only an hour or so before seemed impossible. Then up she would swoop again into joy.

Soon I saw that Emily was not the only girl Gerald favoured; she was by no means the only one helping him with that household. I saw she was not sure of her position with him. Sometimes she did not go to his house, but stayed with me; and I believed this was because she was trying to "show" him, or even confirm for herself that she still had some independence of will.

From the rumour markets I heard that the young man Gerald was "seducing all those young girls; it is shocking." Funny to hear all those old words, "seduce," "immoral," "shocking," and so on; and that they had no force in them was proved by the fact that nothing was done. When citizens are moved one way or another, they show it, but no one really cared much that young women of thirteen, fourteen had sexual relations. We had returned to an earlier time of man's condition.

And what was Emily feeling now? Again, her emotions

had not accommodated change. Only a few weeks, even days, after it was past, she saw herself as the widow of a dead bliss, a paradise: she would have liked that time to have gone on for ever when she felt herself to be a sun drawing everybody in towards her, when she shed light and warmth on them, a joy which she manufactured with her lover, Gerald. But not finding herself first, or alone, with him, finding herself uncertain and unsupported there where she felt her centre to be, she lost her bloom, her lustre; she became peaked, she sat about listlessly, and had to force herself up into activity. I was pleased that this had happened: I could not help it. I still felt she should be with me, because that man—guardian, protector, or whatever he was—had asked me to care for her. And if she was being let down by Gerald—which was how she felt it— then this was painful, but at least she would not go off with him when he took his turn to lead off a tribe. If he now would leave at all, having made this new community.

I waited, watched. . . . Walking through a light screen of leaves, flowers, birds, blossom, the essence of woodland brought to life in the effaced patterns of the wallpaper, I moved through rooms that seemed to have aged since I saw them last. The walls had thinned, had lost substance to the air, to time; everywhere on the forest floor stood slight tall walls, all upright still and in their proper pattern of angles, but ghosts of walls, like the flats in a theatre. They soared into boughs, lost themselves in leaves; and the sunlight lay shallow and clear on them where the leafy shadow patterns did not. Earth had blown in, and fresh grass and flowers grew everywhere.

I walked from room to room through the unsubstantial walls, looking for their occupant, their inhabitant, the one whose presence I could feel strongly, even now when the forest had almost taken the place over.

Someone . . . yes, indeed, there was somebody. Close . . .
I walked soft over the grass along the slant of an eggshell wall
making not a sound, knowing that at the end, where the inter-
secting wall had fallen and decayed long ago, I would easily
and at last turn my head and see—whoever it was . . . a strong
soft presence, an intimate, whose face would be known to me,
had always been known to me. But, when I came to the end of
the wall, a small stream lay bubbling there through the grass,
so clear that the fishes on their ground of bright pebbles looked
up with their round eyes at me as if there was no water between
me and them, as if they hung in air at my feet.

Straying through room after room all open to the leaves
and the sky, floored with the unpoisoned grasses and flowers
of the old world, I saw how extensive was this place, with no
boundaries or end that I could find, much larger than I had
ever understood. Long ago, when it had stood up thick and
strong, a protection from the forest and from the weather, how
very many must have lived here, multitudes, yet all had been
subdued to the one Presence who was the air they breathed—
though they did not know it—was the Whole they were minuscule parts of, their living and their dying as little their personal choice or wanting as the fates and fortunes of molecules
in a leaf are theirs.

I walked back again, towards the border region on whose
other side was my "real" life, and found that here was a set of
rooms still solid, still unthinned, with floors and ceilings intact,
but as I looked I saw how the floorboards were beginning to
give, had collapsed in some places; then that there were ragged
holes in them; then that in fact these were not really floorboards, but only a few rotting planks lying about on earth that
was putting out shoots of green. I pulled the planks away, ex-
posing clean earth and insects that were vigorously at their

work of re-creation. I pulled back heavy lined curtains to let
the sunlight in. The smell of growth came up strong from the
stuffy old room, and I ran from there and pushed my way
back through fine leafy screens, leaving that place, or realm,
to clean growth and working insects because—I had to. After
all, it was never myself who ordained that now I must inter-
rupt my ordinary life, since it was time to step from one life
into another; not I who thinned the sunlight wall; not I who
set the stage behind it. I had never had a choice. Very strong
was the feeling that I did as I was bid and as I must; that I
was being taken, was being led, was being shown, was held
always in the hollow of a great hand which enclosed my life,
and used me for purposes I was too much beetle or earthworm
to understand.

Because of this feeling, born of the experiences behind
the wall, I was changing. A restlessness, a hunger that had been
with me all my life, that had always been accompanied by a
rage of protest (but against what?) was being assuaged. I
found that I was more often simply waiting. I watched to see
what would happen next. I observed. I looked at every new
event quietly, to see if I could understand it.

□  □  □

What happened next was June.

One afternoon, when Emily had been home with me and
Hugo a full day and a night, had not gone at all to the communal household, a little girl came to the door asking for her.
I say "a little girl" conscious of the absurdity of the phrase with
its associations of freshness and promise. But, after all, she was

one: a very thin child, with strong prominent bones. Her eyes were pale blue. She had pale hair that looked dirty hanging to her shoulders and half hiding an appealing little face. She was small for her age, could have been eight or nine, but was in fact eleven. In other words, she was two years younger than Emily, who was a young woman and loved—precariously—by the king, Gerald. But her breasts were stubby little points, and her body altogether in the chrysalis stage.

"Where is Emily?" she demanded. Her voice—but I shall only say that it was at the extreme away from "good English," the norm once used for announcements, news, or by officialdom. I could hardly understand her, her accent was so degraded. I am not talking about the words she used, which were always sharp enough when one had uncoded them, were stubborn and strong attempts to lay hold of meanings and ideas every bit as clear and good as those expressed in tutored speech. The peremptoriness of the "Where is Emily?" was not from rudeness, but because of the effort she had to put into it, the determination to be understood and to be led to Emily or that Emily should be brought out to her. It was, too, because she was a person who had not been brought up to believe she had rights. Yet she set herself towards goals: she wanted things and achieved them; she would reach her Emily without the help of words, skills, manners—without rights.

"She's here," I said. "And please come in."

She followed me, stiff with the determination that had got her here. Her eyes were everywhere, and the thought came into my mind that she was pricing what she saw. Or, rather, valuing, since "pricing" was somewhat out-of-date.

When she saw Emily, today a languid suffering young woman on a chair by the window, her two bare feet set side by side on her attendant yellow beast, the child's face lit with a heartbreakingly sweet smile all confidence and love, and she ran forward, forgetting herself. And Emily, seeing her, smiled and forgot her troubles—love troubles and goodness knows what else, and the two girls went into the tiny room that was Emily's. Two girls in a young girls' friendship, despite one being already a woman, and one still a child, with a child's face and body. But not, as I discovered, with a child's imaginings, for she was in love with Gerald. And, after having suffered jealousy because of the favourite Emily, by turns hating and denigrating her or feverishly and slavishly admiring her, now she was her sister in sorrow when Gerald was being loved, served, by another girl, or girls.

It was morning when she came; and at lunchtime the two emerged from the bedroom and Emily asked, with her unfailing visitor's manners, "If you don't mind, I would like to ask June to have a sandwich or something."

Later in the day, the two tired of the stuffy room and came into the living-room, and sat on the floor on either side of Hugo and talked while they patted and petted him. June was wanting advice and information on all kinds of practical matters, and particularly about the garden, which was Emily's responsibility, since Emily understood about all that kind of thing.

She did? *I* knew nothing of this in Emily, who with me had not showed the slightest interest in such matters, not even in the potted plants.

I sat listening to their talk, reconstructing from it the life of their community. . . . How very odd it was that all over our cities—side by side with citizens who still used electric light, drew water, for which they had paid, from taps, expected their rubbish to be collected—were these houses which were as if the technological revolution had never occurred at all. The big house fifteen minutes' walk away had been an old people's home. It had large grounds. Shrubs and flowerbeds had been cleared and now there were only vegetables. There was even a little shed in which a few fowls were kept—another illegality that went on everywhere, and to which the authorities turned a blind eye. The household bought—or acquired in some way— flour, dried legumes, honey. But they were about to get a hive of bees. They also bought the substitutes "chicken" and "beef" and "lamb" and concocted the usual unappetising meals with them. Unappetising only to some: there were plenty of young people who had eaten nothing else in their lives, and who now preferred the substitute to the real thing. As I've said, we learn to like what we get.

The place was a conglomeration of little workshops: they made soap and candles and wove materials and dyed them; they cured leather; they dried and preserved food; they reconstructed and made furniture.

And so they all lived, Gerald's gang, thirty of them now, with pressure always on them to expand, since so many people wanted to join but had to be refused: there was no space.

It was not that I was surprised to learn of all this. I had heard it all before in various forms. For instance, there had been a community of young adults and small children not far away where even the water system and sewage had broken down. They had made a privy in the garden, a pit with a packing-case over it, and a can of ashes for the smell and the flies. They bought water from the door, or tapped the mains as they could, and cadged baths from friends: there was a time when my bathroom was being used by them. But that group drifted off somewhere. All over our city were these pockets of life reverting to the primitive, the hand-to-mouth. Part of a house . . . then the whole house . . . a group of houses . . . a street . . . an area of streets. People looking down from a high building saw how these nuclei of barbarism took hold and spread. At first the observers were all sharp hostility and fear. They made the sounds of disapproval, of rectitude, but they were in fact learning as they, the still fortunate, watched these savages from whose every finger sprouted new skills and talents. In some parts of the city whole suburbs had reverted. Miles of people, all growing their potatoes and onions and carrots and cabbages and setting guard on them day and night, raising chickens and ducks, making their sewage into compost, buying or selling water, using empty rooms or an empty house to breed rabbits or even a pig—people no longer in neat little families, but huddled together in groups and clans whose structure evolved under the pressures of necessity. At night such an area withdrew itself into a dangerous obscurity where no one dared go, with its spare or absent street lighting, its potholed pavements and rutted streets, the windows showing the minuscule flickering of candles or the shallow glow of some improvised light on a wall or a ceiling. Even in the daytime, to walk there seeing wary faces half-visible behind shutters, knowing that bows and arrows, catapults, or even guns were held trained for use if you transgressed—such an expedition was like a foray into enemy territory, or into the past of the human race.

Yet even at that late stage, there was a level of our society which managed to live as if nothing much was happening— nothing irreparable. The ruling class—but that was a dead phrase, so they said; very well, then, the kind of person who ran things, administered, sat on councils and committees, made decisions. *Talked*. The bureaucracy. An international bureaucracy. But when has it not been true that the section of a society which gets the most out of it maintains in itself, and for as long as it can in others, an illusion of security, permanence, order?

It seems to me that this has something to do, at bottom, with conscience, a vestigial organ in humanity which still demands that there should be some sort of justice or equity; feels that it is intolerable (this *is* felt by most people, somewhere, or at least occasionally) that some people do well while others starve and fail. This is the most powerful of mechanisms for, to begin with, the maintaining of a society, and then its undermining, its rotting, its collapse. . . . Yes, of course this is not new, has been going on throughout history, very likely and as far as we know. Has there been a time in our country when the ruling class was not living inside its glass bell of respectability or of wealth, shutting its eyes to what went on outside? Could there be any real difference when this "ruling class" used words like "justice," "fair play," "equity," "order," or even "socialism"? Used them, might even have believed in them, or believed in them for a time; but meanwhile everything fell to pieces while still, as always, the administrators lived cushioned against the worst, trying to talk away, wish away, legislate away the worst—for to admit that it was happening was to admit themselves useless, admit the extra security they enjoyed was theft and not payment for services rendered. . . .

And yet in a way everybody played a part in this conspiracy that nothing much was happening—or that it was happening, but one day things would go into reverse and hey, presto! back we would be in the good old days. Which, though? That was a matter of temperament: if you have nothing, you are free to choose among dreams and fantasies. I fancied a rather elegant sort of feudalism—without wars, of course, or injustice. Emily, having never experienced or suffered it, would have liked the Age of Affluence back again.

I played the game of complicity like everyone else. I re-

newed my lease during this period, and it was for seven
years: of course I knew that we didn't have anything like that
time left. I remember a discussion with Emily and June about
replacing our curtains. Emily wanted some muslin curtains
in yellow that she had seen in some exchange-shop. I argued
in favour of a thicker material, to keep out noise. June agreed
with Emily: muslin, if properly lined—and there was a stall
that sold nothing but old lining materials only two miles
away—hung well, and was warm. After all, thicker material,
supposedly warmer, hung so stiffly that drafts could get in
around the edges. . . . Yes, but once this thick material had
been washed, it would lose its stiffness. . . . This was the sort
of conversation we were all capable of having; we might spend
days or weeks on a decision. Real decisions, necessary ones,
such as that electricity would have to be given up altogether,
were likely to be made with a minimum of discussion; they
were forced on us—it was that summer that I arranged for
my electricity to be disconnected. Just before June's visit, in
fact. Her first visit. Soon she was coming every day, and usually
found us in discussions about lighting and heating. She told
us that there was a man in a small town about twelve miles
away selling devices of the sort once used for camping. No, they
were not the same devices, but he had evolved all kinds of new
ones: she had seen some; we should get them, too. She and
Emily discussed it, decided not to make the expedition by
themselves, and asked Gerald to go with them. Off they went
and came back late one afternoon loaded with every kind of
gadget and trick for light and heat. And here was Gerald, in
my living-room. From near by, this young chieftain was not
so formidable; he seemed harassed, he was even forlorn—his
continual glances towards Emily had anxiety in them, and he
spent all the time he was there asking for advice about this or

about that. . . . She gave it; she was really extraordinarily practical and sensible. I was seeing something of their relationship—I mean the one beneath that other, perhaps less powerful bond which was evident and on the surface, and to which Emily was responding: beyond this almost conventional business of girl in love with boss of the gang, one saw a very young man, overburdened and over-responsible and unsure, asking for support, even tenderness. He had gone off with Emily and June to "help carry supplies in for Emily and her friend for the winter," but this was not only kindheartedness—he had plenty of that—but a way of saying to Emily that he needed her back in his household. A payment, perhaps; a bribe, if you want to be cynical. Robustly tired after the long walk carrying such a load, looking flushed and sunburned and pretty, she coquetted with him, made herself scarce and difficult. As for June, not yet able to play this game, she was quiet, watching, very much excluded. Emily, feeling power over Gerald, was using it; she stretched, and luxuriated in her body, and played with Hugo's head and ears and smiled at Gerald. . . . Yes, she would go back with him to his house, since he so much wanted it, wanted *her*. And after an hour or so of it, off they went, the three of them, Emily and Gerald first, June tagging on behind. Parents and a child was what it looked like—what it felt like, I guessed, at least to June.

And now I suppose it must be asked and answered why Emily did not choose to be a chieftainess, a leader on her own account? Well, why not? Yes, I did ask myself this, of course. The attitudes of women towards themselves and to men, the standards women had set up for themselves, the gallantry of their fight for equality, the decades-long and very painful questioning of their roles, their functions—all this makes it difficult for me now to say, simply, that Emily was in love.

Why did she not have her own band, her own household of brave foragers and pilferers, of makers and bakers and growers of their own food? Why was it not she of whom it was said, "There was that house, it was standing empty, Emily has got a gang together, and they've moved in. Yes, it's very good there; let's see if she will let us come, too."

There was nothing to stop her. No law, written or un- written, said she should not, and her capacities and talents were every bit as varied as Gerald's or anybody else's. But she did not. I don't think it occurred to her.

The trouble was, she did love Gerald; and this longing for him, for his attention and his notice, the need to be the one who sustained and comforted him, who connected him with the earth, who held him steady in her common sense and her warmth—this need drained her of the initiative she would need to be a leader of a commune. She wanted no more than to be the leader of the commune's woman. His only woman, of course.

This is a history, after all, and I hope a truthful one.


□   □   □


One afternoon I returned from a news-gathering excur- sion and found my rooms had been disturbed, and in exactly the same way as the place behind the wall might be disturbed by the "poltergeist," or anarchic principle. This was my thought as I stood there looking at a chair overturned, books spilled on the floor. There was a general disorder, an emptiness, and, above all, an alien feel to the place. Then, one by one, specific lacks and absences became evident. Supplies of food had gone, stocks of valuable cereals, tinned goods, dried fruits; candles, skins, polythene sheeting—the obvious things. Very well, then —thieves had broken in, and I was lucky it had not happened before. But then I saw that possessions only retrospectively valuable were missing: a television set unused for months, a tape recorder, electric lamps, a food mixer. The city had warehouses full of electric contrivances no longer useful for anything, and I began to think that these thieves were freakish or silly. I saw that Hugo lay stretched in his place along the outer wall; he had not been disturbed by the intruders. This was strange, and no sooner had I become convinced of the inexplicable nature of this robbery than the sound of voices I knew well took me to the window. There I stood to watch a little procession of the goods being brought back again. On a dozen heads, children's heads, were balanced the television, sacks of fuel and food, all sorts of bags and boxes. The faces became visible, brown and white and black, when they tilted up in response to Emily's voice: "There, now, we're too late," meaning that I was back and stood at the window watching. I saw Emily coming behind the others. She was in charge: supervising, looking responsible, annoyed—officious. I had not seen her in this role before; this was a new Emily to me. June was there, too, beside Emily. I knew all these faces—the children were from Gerald's household.

In a moment, boxes, bundles, and cases were filing into my living-room, the children beneath them. When the floor was covered with what had been taken, the children began to edge out again, looking at Emily but never at me: I might as well have been invisible.

"And now say you're sorry," she ordered.

They smiled, the feeble awkward smile that goes with *Oh, how she does go on!* They were obeying Emily, but she

was found overbearing: those embarrassed, affectionate smiles
were not the first she had wrung out of them, I could see. I
became even more curious about her role in that other house.

"No, come on," said Emily. "It's the least you can do."

June's thin shoulders shrugged, and she said, "We are
sorry. But we have brought them back, haven't we?" My
attempt to transcribe this is: "Aow, w'srry, 't wiv brung'm beck,
ivnt wee?"

In this effort of speech was the energy of frustration: this
child, like others formed by our old time which above all had
been verbal—to do with words, the exchange of them, the use
of them—had been excluded from all that richness. We (meaning the educated) had never found a way of sharing that
plenty with the lower reaches of our society. Even in two
women standing on a street's edge bartering their few sentences
of gossip had been the explosive effort of frustration: the deprived, thinned speech of the poor had always had somewhere
in it the energy of a resentment (unconscious, perhaps, but
there) fed by the knowledge of skills and ease just beyond
them, and whose place in their talk was taken by the constant
repetition of the phrases—like crutches—"you know?" and
"you know what I mean?" and "isn't it?" and all the rest,
phrases which made up a good part of everything they said.
Words in their mouths—now in June's—had a labouring
effortful quality—dreadful because of the fluencies so easily
available, but to others.

The children went off at last, June lingering behind. From
her look around the room, I could see she did not want to go.
She was regretting not the act but the consequences of it, which
might sever her from her beloved Emily.

"What was that about?" I asked.

Emily's bossiness dropped from her, and she slumped, a
worried and tired child, near Hugo. He licked her cheek.

"Well, they fancied some of your things, that's all."

"Yes, but . . ." My feeling was *But I'm a friend and they shouldn't have picked on me!* Emily caught this, and with her dry little smile she said, "June had been here, she knew the lay-out, so when the kids were wondering what place to do next, she suggested yours."

"Makes sense, I suppose."

"Yes," she insisted, raising serious eyes to me, so that I shouldn't make light of her emphasis. "Yes, it does make sense."

"You mean, I shouldn't think there was anything personal in it?"

Again the smile, pathetic because of its knowingness, its precocity—but what an old-fashioned word that was, depending for its force on certain standards.

"Oh, no, it was personal . . . a compliment, if you like!"

She put down her face into Hugo's yellow fur and laughed. I knew she needed to hide her face from the effort of presenting it all bright and eager, good and clever. Her two worlds, Gerald's place, my place, had overlapped in a threatening way. I could feel that in her, understand it. But there was an exhaustion in her, a strain that I did not understand—though I believed I had caught a glimpse of the reason in her relations with the children. Was her problem not so much that she was only one of the contenders for Gerald's favour, but that the burdens on her were much too heavy for someone her age?

I asked, "Why did they bother with the electrical goods?"

"Because they were there," she replied, over-short; and I knew she was disappointed in me. I had not understood the differences between *them*—a category in which she sometimes did and sometimes did not include herself—and me.

Now she was looking at me. Not without affection, I'm

glad to say, but it was quizzical. She was wondering whether
to attempt something with me. If it would be resented? Would
be understood?

She said, "Have you been upstairs recently?"

"No, I suppose not. Should I have?"

"Well, then—yes, yes, I think you should!" And as she
made up her mind to go ahead with whatever it was, she became whimsical, gay, a little girl charming or disarming a
parent or adult. She cried out, "But we must find something
to put things on—yes, this will do. And of course if the lift
isn't working—and most of the time it isn't these days—oh,
dear!"

In a moment she was flying about the rooms, gathering
together every electrical object I had, except for the radio,
without which we were still convinced we could not live—the
news from other countries might just as well be from other
planets, so far away did they seem now; and in any case, things
went on there just the same as they did with us. Mixers, the
television, lamps—these I have already mentioned. To these
were added a hair dryer, a massager, a grill, a toaster, a roaster,
a coffee-pot, a kettle, a vacuum cleaner. They were all piled
together on a double-layered trolley.

"Come, come, come, come," she cried gaily, gently, her
serious eyes ever on me for fear I might be taking offence,
and out we went, pushing the overloaded trolley. The hall was
full of people: they streamed up and down the stairs, or waited
for the lift, which was working; they laughed and talked and
shouted. It was a crowd alight and aglitter, restless, animated,
fervent; everyone looked as if he or she had a fever. Now I
realised that of course I had become used to seeing the hall
and the pavement immediately outside the building full of
this crowd, but I had not understood. This was because along

the corridors of the lower floors of the building, all was as it had been: quietness, sobriety, and doors marked 1, 2, 3, behind which lived Mr. and Mrs. Jones and family, Miss Foster and Miss Baxter, Mr. and Mrs. Smith and Miss Alicia Smith—little self-contained units, the old world.

We waited for our turn for the lift, pushed the loaded trolley into it, and went up with a crush of people who glanced at our goods and did not think much of them. On the top floor we pushed the trolley into the passage, and Emily stood for a moment undecided. I could see it was not because she did not know her way, but because she was working out what would be best for me: precisely, what would be *good* for me!

Up here it was the same as on the ground floor: rooms all round the building with a corridor behind them; single rooms off that, a court in the middle—but here the court was of course a well, or gulf. There was a great bustle and movement up here, too. Doors stood open everywhere. It was like the approach to a street market: people with bundles of goods in their arms, or an old pram loaded with this or that, a man carefully holding a wrapped precious thing above his head so that no one could bump into it. It was hard to remember that in the lower parts of the building was quiet and the sense of people giving each other space. A room opposite the lift had a great mound of stuff, right up to the ceiling, and around it crouched children sorting things out into their categories. A child smiled up at Emily and explained, "I'm just helping with this load; it's just come in," and Emily said, "That's good, I'm glad," reassuring the child. Again, there was in this exchange something which made me wonder: the little girl had been over-ready to explain herself. But we were in the entrance to another room, where an irregular gap in the wall, like bomb damage, communicated with the room we had left—the heap

of things had hidden the gap. Through it were being taken
by hand, or trundled on various kinds of little cart, certain
categories of goods: this room was for containers—jars, bottles,
cans, and so on, and they were in every sort of material, from
glass to cardboard. About a dozen children were at the work
of carrying the containers from the heap next door, through
the gap, into this room: the one thing these markets were not
short of, the one commodity no one had been short of for a
long time, was labour, was hands to work at whatever was
needed. In the corner stood two youths on guard, with
weapons: guns, knives, knuckle-dusters. It was not until we
stood outside the door of yet another room, where the atmosphere was altogether lower, and more listless, and where there
was no guard, that I understood the contents of the rooms with
the two armed boys were valuable, but that this room held
stuff not valued at all: electrical goods like those we were
pushing on our trolley.

We stood there for a while watching the bustle and movement, watching the children at work.

"They get money, you see," said Emily. "Or get something
in exchange—even the kids at school come here for an hour or
so."

And I saw that indeed among these children, some of
whose faces were familiar enough, from the pavement, were
some better-dressed, cleaner, but above all with that wary
self-contained I'm-only-here-on-my-own-terms look that dis-
tinguishes the youngsters of a privileged class when engaged in
work that is beneath their conception of themselves. They were
here, in short, doing the equivalent of the holiday tasks of
middle-class children in the old days—packing goods for firms,
cleaning in restaurants, selling behind the counter. Yes, I could
have noticed this without Emily, in time; but her shrewd eyes

were on me hastening the process; she really was finding me slow to take in, to adapt, and when I did not seem to have understood as quickly as she thought I should, she set herself to explain. It seemed that as people left these upper floors empty to flee from the city, dealers had moved in. It was a large building, much heavier and better-built than most, with good thick floors that could take weight. Mr. Mehta had bought rights in a rubbish dump before the government had commandeered all rubbish dumps, and was in business with various people: one was Gerald's father, a man who had once run a business making cosmetics. Usable stuff from the dump was brought here, and sorted out, mostly by children. People came up here to trade. A lot of the goods were taken down again to the street markets and shops.

Goods that were broken and could be mended were put right here: we passed rooms where skilled people, mostly older ones, sat and mended gadgets, broken saucepans, clothes, furniture. There was in these rooms a great liveliness and interest: people stood around watching. An old man, a watchmender, sat in a corner under a light specially rigged up for him, and around him, fascinated, hardly drawing breath, pressed in a thick crowd—so thick that a guard kept asking them to stand back and, when they did not, held them with a cudgel. They hardly noticed this, so intent were they, old and young, men and women, on watching this precious skill—an old man's hands at work in the tiny machinery.

There was a woman fitting lenses to spectacle frames. She had an oculist's chart on the wall and, according to its findings, was handing out secondhand spectacles to people who stood in a line and who each took from her a pair that she considered suitable. An oculist from the old days; and she, too, had a crowd of admirers. A chair-mender, a basket-mender

surrounded with his twisted rushes and reeds, a knife-grinder
—here they all were, the old skills, each with a guard, each
watched by marvelling barbarians.

What wasn't to be seen in the rooms we passed through,
one after another? String and bottles, piles of plastic and polythene pieces (the most valuable, perhaps, of all commodities);
bits of metal, wire flex, plastic tape; books and hats and clothes.
There was a room full of things that seemed quite new and
good which had reached the rubbish dumps shielded from
dirt and spoiling: a jersey in a plastic bag, umbrellas, artificial
flowers, a carton full of corks.

And everywhere the pressing lively people, here as much
for the show as for the goods. There was even a little café in
one room, selling herbal teas, bread, spirits. A lot of people
seemed tipsy, but they often do at markets, without alcohol. It
was hard to tell the sellers from the buyers, the owners from
the visitors; it was a polyglot crowd, a good-natured crowd,
who respected the orders and instructions of the many guards;
an orderly crowd, and one able in the new manner to settle
among themselves disputes and differences quickly and without bad feeling being allowed to fester. People joked, showed
each other their purchases, and even bought and sold from
each other without going to the formality of engaging the
services of the official traders—a process which was quite in
order and approved of. What the traders wanted was a crowd,
was plenty of people, was the flow of goods in and out.

We made a tour of the entire floor, and, having been
greeted by innumerable people—many of the people from the
pavement were up here—again entered the room for electrical
goods and pushed forward our trolley. For this merchandise we
were given a few vouchers, and I said to Emily that since it
was her enterprise that had brought us here, she should have

the spending of the results of it. She looked quizzical again—
I had come to expect this, and understood it was because I
might be expecting too much in the way of a return. And what
would be done, I wanted to know, with our toasters and
roasters? Well, they would be dismantled for their parts, and
these parts would be incorporated into other objects—obviously
they were of no use as they were? Surely I didn't mind seeing
them go? Well, if I didn't mind, she would very much like
to take to Gerald's house—was I sure I didn't mind?—some
stuff for the kitchen, because they were short. We found an
old saucepan, an enamel jug, a plastic bowl, a scrubbing brush:
this was what we got in exchange for the electrical equipment
of what had been, after all, a lavishly equipped flat.

Back in our flat, Emily put off her little-girl charm—without which she could never have brought herself to take me up
on an expedition she clearly felt was into her territory and a
long way from mine—and sat observing me. She was wondering, I suppose, unflattering though that was, if I had really
understood that goods, "things," were different commodities
for her and for children like June; in some ways more precious,
because irreplaceable, but also without value. . . . No, that is
not right, without personal value: things did not belong to
people as they did once. Of course, this had been true among
some people long before the time of getting and having had
passed: all sorts of experiments in communalism had been
worked through, apart from the fact that people like "the
Ryans" had dispensed with ideas of mine and thine, and this
without any theories or ideas about it. June was June Ryan;
her family had been the despair of the authorities long before
the collapse of the old society, when things had still been assumed to be normal. And, as a Ryan . . . But more of this
later, when I describe "the Ryans" in their proper place.

Why am I postponing it? This place will do as well as another. Is my wanting to postpone what for the sake of the narrative has to be said about the Ryans no more than an extension and a reflection of the attitudes and emotions of the said authorities towards "the Ryans"? The point being that "the Ryans," meaning a way of life, were unassimilable, both in theory—theories about society and how it worked—and in practice?

To describe them, their circumstances—nothing here that the reader won't have heard a hundred times: it was a textbook case, as the social workers kept exclaiming. An Irish labourer had married a Polish refugee. Both were Catholics. In due time there were eleven children. He drank, was brutal, was intermittently affectionate. She drank, was hysterical, incompetent, unpredictably loving. The children would not stay in school. Welfare authorities, housing authorities, the police, the psychologists—all knew the Ryans. Then the two older boys were in court for stealing, and went to Borstal for a time. The second—not the oldest—girl got pregnant. She was fifteen. No, there is nothing unfamiliar about any of it, but the Ryans' case seemed to be larger and more hopeless because there were so many of them, and because both parents were large and colourful characters whose sayings were likely to be quoted at conferences and at meetings. It often happens that a single case takes wing out of its anonymity and represents others; in our city alone there were thousands of "Ryans" of all kinds, colours, nations, unknown except to their neighbours and to the authorities, and these people in due time found themselves in prison, Borstal, remand homes, and so on. But some charity interested itself in the Ryan family; they were installed in a house; efforts were made to keep them together.

This was how the picture looked to officialdom doing as

well as it could; how it looked in reports; how a newspaper, choosing the Ryans out of so many because of this quality they had of being more visible than others, presented them. *Below the Poverty Line and Lower,* this was called. A book recording a dozen cases, the Ryans among them, was *Rejects of the Affluent Society.* A young man just out of university, whose aunt was a welfare worker on the case, had collected notes for a book, *The Barbarians We Make,* comparing the Ryans to those who pulled down Rome from its heights.

How about the Ryan house, for a start? Well, it was filthy, and what furniture it had fit for a rubbish dump. Nothing on the bare floors but dirt, a bone, a plate of rancid cat's food: dogs and cats, like children, were fed impulsively. There was never much heat, so the thirteen Ryans and their friends— the Ryans attracted others and kept them in orbit—were always in one room, huddling. The parents were usually drunk and sometimes the children were, too. The friends were all colours, and often remarkable, with lives out of the ordinary, and they all sat about eating biscuits or chips, and talking, talking; but sometimes the mother or an older girl cooked up some potatoes with a bit of meat, or opened some tins of something, and it became a festival. Chips and sweet drinks and tea with six or eight spoons of white sugar to each cup—such was the diet of the Ryans, so they were always listless, or on some unnatural peak of vitality while the sugar jigged in their arteries. They sat and talked and talked; the room was lively with that perpetually renewed chronicle, *The Ryans Against the World.* How the three middle children had been set on in the playground by a rival gang or family, but had won; or how the welfare woman had left a piece of paper saying that the fifth child, Mary, had to go to the clinic on Wednesday, and really must try to remember this time, for her rash ought to be at-

tended to; how Paul had found a car unlocked and had taken
—whatever was there, because it was there. Two of the girls
had visited a chain store and had come back with twenty small
plastic purses, two pounds of coffee, gardening shears, some
spices from the Indian shelf, and six plastic cullenders. These
articles would lie about unused, or might be bartered for other
objects: the thieving was for the sake of the act, not of possession. The black girl Tessa, Ruth's friend, and Tessa's brother,
and Ruth's other friend Irene and her sister had watched the
television all the afternoon in one of the friendly television
shops on the main street which did not chase away children
who sidled in for an afternoon's free viewing—the Ryans' set
was always broken. Stephen had met a dog on the street, and
had gone to the canal and thrown sticks for the dog and the
dog was ever so clever; it brought back three—no, five—even
six sticks at once. . . . They talked, they talked, they drank and
made their day, their lives, through vivid shrewd comment;
and when they went to bed, it was three, four, six in the
morning—but they did not undress; no one in that house undressed to go to bed, for it was never bedtime. A child would
drop off where he sat, on his sister's lap, and stay there asleep,
or be set down on the floor on a coat. By morning the four
beds of the house each had three or four bodies in them, with
the dogs and cats, all close together, warm, warming, protecting. No one got up till ten, eleven, mid-afternoon: if a Ryan
found a job, he or she lost it in a week, because it was impossible to get up on time.

They lived on welfare, unless Mr. Ryan aroused himself,
became sober, and found a job: he was a carpenter. Then
money flowed in, and they got clothes and shoes. These garments were worn communally, for no one owned this jersey
or that dress. Children wore what fitted and what lay nearest.

New clothes might easily be in rags the day after they arrived in the house, for some reason or another.

The children went on a "job" when the mood took them, which was often. June, the thin sweet-faced little girl, was leader from the age of about seven. Four or five children would slide their way into a flat or a shop and emerge with—money? No, not so, that was not the point; or if it was money, then their pockets would be stacked for days with wads of notes which would fall out or be given away or "lifted" by someone else. No, they were more likely to return with a marble table lamp, a stack of coffee tables which they had seen in a tele-vision advertisement and fancied the look of, a mirror with a pink plastic frame, and cigarettes—which last were valued and instantly shared out.

The point was, the goal of the saints and philosophers was theirs by birthright: *The Way of the Ryans,* it might be called. Each day, each experience, was sufficient unto itself, each act divorced from its consequences. "If you steal that, you will have to go to prison." "If you don't eat properly, you will suffer from vitamin deficiencies." "If you spend that money now, there won't be any to pay the rent on Friday." These truths, always being presented to them by the officials in and out of the house, could never stay in a Ryan head.

And surely the priests and spiritual preceptors were abashed? To be attached to property is bad? What property? A Ryan had none, not even a shirt or a comb. To be the slave to habit is a chain? What habits—unless to have none is a habit of a kind. Regard thy neighbour as thyself? This grace of the very poor was theirs: within the clan which was the Ryans and their friends—white, black, and brown—who came and went day and night in and out of the house, was infinite giving and tolerance, was a generosity of judgement, a delicacy of understanding not given to many more fortunate people, or at least not without hard jostling with event and circumstance.

One ought not to care for appearances? It was a long time since the Ryans had been able to afford this luxury.

One ought not to be puffed up, should not stand upon one's rights, should be humble and non-demanding? Five minutes in the Ryan household would have any middle-class person indignantly on the telephone to his lawyer.

Feckless and irresponsible, hopeless, futureless, uneducated and ineducable—if they could read and write their names, they did well; debased and depressed and depraved—but what could you expect when four or five people of any sex or age slept together in one bed?—dirty, unhealthy, louse-ridden, and limp with bad feeding when they weren't on a momentary "high" . . . in short and to be done with it, everything that our old society regarded as bad the Ryans were. Everything that our old society aimed at the Ryans did not even attempt: they had opted out; it was all too much for them.

The poor Ryans, doomed and damned; the dangerous Ryans, such a threat to us all, to our ways of thinking; the lucky Ryans, whose minute-by-hour life, communal and hugger-mugger, seemed all enjoyment and sensation: they liked being together. They liked each other.

When the bad times started—or, rather, were *seen* to be starting, a very different thing—the Ryans and all the others like them were suddenly in a different light. First of all—but, of course, this is a sociological cliché—some of the boys found places in the police or one of the many military or semi-military organisations that sprang up. And then, it was these people who took most easily to the hand-to-mouth life in the wandering tribes: nothing very much had changed for them, for when had they not been on the move, from room to broken-down house to council flat to hostel in a squatters' street? They ate badly? They were eating better and more healthily now than when civilisation had fed them. They were ignorant and illiterate? They were surviving capably and with enjoyment, which was more than could be said of so many of the middle-class people, who either lived on pretending that nothing was *really* happening, only a reorganisation of society, or faded away in a variety of ways, not able to bear an existence where respectability and gain could no longer measure the worth of a person.

"The Ryans," no longer an extreme, disappeared into society, were absorbed by it. As for our Ryans, the actual family described here, there was still a nucleus somewhere near, the mother and three of the smaller children: the father had died in an accident to do with drink. All the older children had left the city, except for two in the police. June had attached herself to Gerald's household, and one of her younger brothers was there part of the time. "The Ryans" had turned out to be nothing special, after all. In their humble, non-demanding way they had been part of our society, even when they had seemed not to be: they had been formed by it, were obedient to it. They were as far from what was to come afterwards, and quite soon—when "the gang of kids from the Underground" appeared in our lives and wrecked Gerald's house—as we were, or had been, from "the Ryans."

I use that phrase "Gerald's house" as people had once said "the Ryans," meaning a way of life. Temporary ways of life, both: all of our ways of living, our compromises, our little adaptations—transitory all of them; none could last.

But while they lasted, so much clung to and worked at, like Emily with her duties in Gerald's house. Which I now visited, for Emily and I had not been back in our rooms for more than a few minutes when the doorbell went and it was June, all bright anxious smiles. At first she did not mention the robbery, but sat on the floor with her arms around Hugo. Her eyes were on the move around the room, to see where the things she had taken away and been forced to return, now were. Most were out of sight, back in cupboards and storeplaces, but there was a bundle of fur pieces on a chair, and at last she said, in a spurt of desperate restitution, "That's all right, is it? I mean, it's all right?" And she even got up to pat the fur, as if it were an animal she might have hurt. I would have liked to laugh, or to smile, but Emily was frowning at me, very fierce indeed, and she said gently to June, "Yes, everything is fine, thank you." At which the child brightened up at once, and she said, turning her attention to me with difficulty, "Will you visit us? I mean Gerald says it is all right. I asked him, you see? I said to him, can she come, do you see what I mean?"

"I'd like to very much," I said, having consulted Emily with my eyes. She was smiling: it was the smile of a mother or a guardian.

But first Emily had to prepare herself: she emerged in due time from the bathroom, her hair newly washed and combed down, her clothes neat, her breasts outlined in blue cotton, cheeks soft and fresh and smelling of soap—a tidy package of a girl, all ready to present herself to her responsibilities, to Gerald. But her eyes were sombre, defensive, worried, and there beside her was June the child, and her face was laid open and absolutely undefended in a trustful smile at Emily the woman—her friend.

We walked, the three of us, through streets dusty and as usual littered with paper, cans, every kind of debris. It would be necessary to pass a tall hotel built in tourism's last fling, and I was watching to see the route Emily would choose: every

individual picked out a careful way between hazards in these
streets, and one could tell a good deal about a person's nature
by whether she chose to go past a dubious building, taking a
chance she might be seen from it as prey or target, or move
into another street altogether; by whether she boldly called
greetings into defended gardens or walked past quickly with
an averted face. Emily went direct, walking carelessly through
all the rubbish. Not for the first time I marvelled at the different standards for in and out of doors: inside her home, Emily
was as pernickety as a little cat, but outside she seemed not to
see what she walked through.

The hotel had been taken over by squatters long ago: another obsolete word. But all kinds of people lived there, although as a machine the place was useless, like all the
complicated buildings which had depended on technicalities.

I looked up the tall shaft, today outlined against an
over-hot and dusty sky; it showed ragged and patched, like
lace: windows had been smashed or blown in. Yet the upper
parts of it bristled everywhere with devices. Outside one
window would be a whirr of light—someone had rigged up
a little windmill for catching wind and turning it into power
for hot water or lighting. Outside others were slanting discs
held out on what looked from down in the street like spider
webs: these were solar snares of various kinds. And among
these up-to-the-minute contraptions danced and dangled coloured washing held out into the air on timeless string and
wood.

Up there it looked gay and even frivolous, with the blue
sky as backdrop; down here rubbish was banked up all
around the building, with pathways cleared through it to the
doors. The smell—but I'll ignore that, as Emily and June
seemed able to do so easily.

Recently I had gone into the building, had gone up to the very top: there I stood looking down over the city which—I suppose not surprisingly—did not *look* so very different from as it did in the years before the machines stopped working. I had gazed down and fancied myself back in time: all of us did this a great deal, matching and comparing, balancing facts in our minds to make them fit, to orient ourselves against them. The present was so remarkable and dreamlike that to accommodate it meant this process had to be used: *It was like that, was it? Yes, it was like that, but now . . .* As I stood up there, thinking that there was one thing missing, an aeroplane, a jet rising up or descending to the airport and dominating the sky, I heard a soft droning, a bee's sound, no louder, and there it was—a plane. A little one, like a grasshopper, painted bright red, all alone in the empty sky where once so many great machines had filled our lives with noise. There it was, a survivor, holding perhaps the police or the army or high officials off to some conference somewhere to talk, talk, talk, and pass resolutions about our situation, the sad plight of people everywhere in the world. It was pretty to look at; it lifted the spirits to see that little thing glittering up there in emptiness, off to some place which no one looking up at it could get near these days except in imagination.

I had walked slowly down through the erstwhile hotel, exploring, examining. I had been reminded of a new township built for African labourers outside a large mine in Africa that I saw in the, after all, not-so-long-ago days when the continents were close together, were a day's journey away. The township covered acres, had been built all at one time, and was made of thousands of identical little "houses," each consisting of one room and a small kitchen, a lavatory with a wash-basin. But in one house you would see the pattern of tribal village

life brought to the town almost unchanged: a fire burned in
the centre of the brick floor, a roll of blankets stood in a
corner, and two saucepans and a mug in another. In the next
"house" a scene of Victorian respectability: a sideboard, dining
table, a bed, all in hideous varnish, with a dozen crocheted
articles for ornament, and a picture of Royalty on the wall opposite the entrance so that the Queen, in full military regalia,
and the observer could exchange glances of approval over this
interior. In between these extremes was every variation and
compromise. Well, that was what this hotel had become: it was
a set of vertical streets in which you could find everything,
from a respectably clean family making jokes about conditions
in England before the advent of proper sewage disposal and
carrying chamber-pots and pails down flight after flight of
stairs to the one lavatory that still worked, to people living,
eating, sleeping on the floor, who burned fuel on a sheet of
asbestos and pissed out of the window—a faint spray descending
from the heavens these days need not mean imminent rain or
condensing steam.

From the possibility of which event I wanted to hurry on
and away, instead of standing there, among rubbish, gazing
up; particularly as I could see through the windows of the
ground floor a couple of young men with guns. They guarded
the building, or part of it, or just their own room, or rooms—
who knew? But June, seeing them, exclaimed and called out
and looked pleased—in the way she had of being pleased, as
if every little event offered her undeserved riches of pleasure.
With an apology to Emily for keeping her waiting (*my* presence she had the greatest difficulty in remembering at all), in
she went, while we two, Emily and I, stood there in a cloud of
flies, watching a scene through a window of June being embraced and embracing—one of the two young men had visited

in the Ryan house, which meant he had been almost part of the family. Now he gave her a dozen pigeons: the guns were air-guns; the pigeons would come back—they had flown off as we arrived—and settle again over the rubbish where they had been feeding. We left, carrying the dead birds which would do for the household's next meal, hearing the silken whirring of many wings, and the pop, pop, pop of the air-guns.

We crossed old railway lines, flourishing now with plants, some of which Emily pulled up, as she passed, for medicine and flavourings. Soon we were at the side of the house. Yes, I had walked past it, out of curiosity, in my walks, but had never wanted to go in, fearing as always to encroach on Emily. Again June waved at a youth standing behind ground-floor shutters that were half-open because of the heat, and again some weapon or other was put aside. We entered into a room which was very bare and clean—this struck me first of all, for I had not shed old associations with "the Ryans." No furniture at all, but there were curtains, and the shutters were scrubbed and whole, and mats and mattresses were rolled and stood along the walls. I was being taken from room to room on a rapid tour, while I looked for the communal rooms—dining-room, sitting-room, and so on. There was a long room for eating, with trestles and benches, everything scrubbed bare, but otherwise each room was self-sufficient as a workroom or as a home. We opened door after door on groups of children sitting on mattresses which were also beds; they were talking, or engaged on some task, and on the walls were hung clothes and belongings. It could be seen that natural affinities and alliances had made, were making, of this community a series of smaller groups.

There was a kitchen, a large room where half of the floor had been covered with asbestos sheets and then corrugated-iron sheets where fires of whatever fuel was available could burn.

There was a fire burning now, and a meal being prepared by two youngsters, who, when they saw it was Emily, stood aside to let her taste and examine: it was a stew, made of meat substitute with potatoes. She said it was good, but what about a few herbs, and offered them the handfuls she had gathered off the railway lines. And here were some pigeons: they could pluck them if they liked, or otherwise find somebody who would like an extra task—no; she, Emily, would find someone and send them to do it.

I understood now what I had half noticed before—the way the children reacted when they saw Emily. This was how people respond to Authority. And now, because she had criticised the stew, a boy knelt and chopped the greenstuff on a board with a piece of sharpened steel: he had been given an order, or so he felt, and was obeying her.

Emily's eyes were on me: she wanted to know what I had seen, what I made of it, what I was thinking. She looked so worried that June instinctively put her hand into Emily's and smiled at her; all this was such a sharp little presentation of a situation that I did not avoid it by pretending I had noticed nothing.

Only a few days before, Emily had come in late from this household, and had said to me, "It is impossible not to have a pecking order. No matter how you try not to." And she had been not far off tears—and a little girl's tears, at that.

And I said, "You aren't the first person to have that difficulty!"

"Yes, but it isn't what we meant, what we planned. Gerald and I talked it over, right at the start; it was all discussed; there wasn't going to be any of that old nonsense, people in charge telling people what to do, all that *horrible* stuff."

I had said to her, "Everybody has been taught to find a

place in a structure—that as a first lesson. To obey. Isn't that so? And so that is what everybody does."

"But most of these children have never had any education at *all*."

She was all indignation and incredulity. A grown-up—a very grown-up and responsible—question she was asking: after all, it is one that most adults never ask. But what had confronted me there had been a young girl in whose eyes kept appearing—only to be driven down, fought down—the needs of a child for reassurance, the sullen reproach against circumstances of a very young person, not an adult at all.

"It starts when you are born," I said. " 'She's a good girl. She's a bad girl. Have you been a good girl today? I hear you've been a bad girl. Oh, she's so *good,* such a good child.' . . . *Don't you remember?*" She had stared at me; she had not really heard. "It's all false, it's got to do with nothing real, but we are all in it all our lives—you're a good little girl, you're a bad little girl. 'Do as I tell you and I'll tell you you are good.' It's a trap and we are all in it."

"We *decided* it wasn't going to happen," she said.

"Well," I had said, "you don't get a democracy by passing resolutions or thinking democracy is an attractive idea. And that's what we have always done. On the one hand, 'you're a good little girl, a bad little girl,' and institutions and hierarchies and a place in the pecking order; and on the other, passing resolutions about democracy, or saying how democratic we are. So there is no reason for you to feel so bad about it. All that has happened is what always happens."

She had got to her feet: she was angry, confused, impatient with me.

"Look," she said. "We had everything so that we could make a new start. There was no need to get like it's got. That's the point, I'm afraid." And she had gone off to the kitchen, to get away from the subject.

And now here she was, standing in the kitchen of her— or Gerald's—household, angry, flushed, resentful.

That child there, hurrying over his task, not looking up because the overseer still stood there and might criticise—this humiliated her. "But *why*," she whispered staring at me, really —I could see—wanting an answer, an explanation. And June stood smiling there beside her, not understanding but gazing in pity at her poor friend who was so upset.

"Oh, all right, never mind!" said Emily at last, turning away from me, June, the scene, and going out, but asking as she went, "Where's Gerald? He said he would be here."

"He went with Maureen to the market," said one of the children.

"He didn't leave a message?"

"He said we must tell you that we must have our heads done today."

"Oh, he did, did he!" But then, already relieved of her distress, she said, "Right, tell everyone to get to the hall." And she led the way to the garden.

It was a fine garden in every way, planned, prepared, organised, full of good things, all for use—potatoes, leeks, onions, cabbages, the lot—and not a weed or a flower in sight. Some children were at work there, and as they saw Emily they quickened their pace.

Suddenly she exclaimed, "Oh, no, no, I said the spinach should be left until next week, it's being over-picked." A child of about seven quite openly grimaced at June—it was that face which is made to say, *Who does she think she is, bossing us?* —that absolutely routine reaction, to be observed in one form or another anywhere there are groups, hierarchies, institutions.

In short, everywhere. But Emily saw it, suffered, and softened her voice: "But I did say leave it, didn't I? Can't you see for yourself? The leaves are still tiny."

"I'll show Pat," said June quickly.

"It doesn't matter, really," said Emily.

Before we left the garden, Emily had again to exclaim and explain: wood ash from the fires to control fly on the cabbages had been laid too close around the stems. "Can't you *see?*" said Emily to the child—a black child, this time, who stood rigid in front of her, his face agonised with the effort of taking this criticism when he felt he was doing so well. "It shouldn't be close to the stem; you should make a circle, like this. . . ." And she knelt down on the damp soil and trickled ash out of a plastic bag around the cabbage stem. She did it neatly and quickly, she was so expert; and the child sighed and looked at June, who put her arm around him. When Emily looked up from her task with the ash, she saw the two children, one in the protective embrace of the other, allied against her, the boss. She went scarlet, and said, "I'm sorry if I spoke sharply, I didn't mean to." At which both children, disengaging themselves from each other, fell in on either side of her and went, distressed by her distress, through the paths of that exemplary garden, towards the house. I followed, forgotten. The black child had put his hand on Emily's forearm; June had hold of her other hand; Emily was walking blind between them, and I knew this was because her eyes were full of tears.

At the back door she went ahead by herself, the black child following. June fell back to be with me. She smiled at me, really seeing me for this one time: her shy, open, defenceless smile offered me her inadequacy, her deprivation—her history. At the same time, her eyes asked that I should not criticise Emily, for she could not bear Emily to be disliked.

In the hall, or dining-room, the trestles had bowls of water set all along them that smelled of a strong herb; there were fine combs and bits of old cloth. Beside the trestles stood the children, and the older ones, with Emily, began to comb through the offered scalps.

Emily had forgotten me. Then she saw me and called, "Would you like to stay and eat with us?"

But I could see she did not want me to.

I had scarcely turned to take myself off when I heard her anxiety ring out: "Did Gerald say when he would be back? Did Maureen say anything? Surely he said something about how long they would be?"

Back in my home, I saw, through the window, Gerald arriving on the pavement with a girl, presumably Maureen, and there he stood surrounded as usual with the younger children, some from his household, some not. He probably saw his loitering there for hours at a time as a function. I suppose it was. Collecting information as we all had to; attracting new recruits for his household (but he had more applicants than he could take in); simply showing himself there, displaying his qualities among the four or five other young men who were the natural leaders—was this the equivalent of a male going out to hunt while the women kept themselves busy at home? I entertained these thoughts as I stood with Hugo beside me, watching the young man in his brigand's outfit prominent among the people there, with so many young girls hanging about, catching his eye, waiting to talk to him . . . old thoughts, about stale social patterns. Yet one had them, they did not die. Just as the old patterns kept repeating themselves, re-forming themselves even when events seemed to license any experiment or deviation or mutation, so did the old thoughts, which matched the patterns. I kept hearing Emily's shrill, over-pressured voice: "Where's Gerald, where is he?" as she stood in her woman's place, combing nits and lice out of the younger children's heads, while Gerald was probably planning some expedition to capture supplies from somewhere, for no one could say of him that he was unresourceful or lazy.

Later he was gone from the pavement, and Maureen, too. Soon after that, Emily came home. She was very tired and did not try to conceal it. She sank down at once beside the animal, and rested there while I made the supper. I served it, and washed up while she rested again. It seemed to me that my visiting that other house, and seeing how much she had to do there, enabled her at last to relax with me, to sit and allow herself to be served by me. When I finished the washing-up, I made us both a cup of tea, and sat with her on into the dusk of that summer evening while she sat limp beside her Hugo.

Outside, the noise and clamour of the pavement under a colourful sunset. In here was quiet, a soft light, the purring of the animal as he licked Emily's forearm. In here, the sound of a girl crying, like a child, with small fastidious sniffs and gulps. She did not want me to know she was crying but did not care enough to move away.

The wall opened. Behind it was an intensely blue sky, a blue sharply clear and cold, blue that never was in nature. From horizon to horizon the sky stood uniformly filled with colour, and with nowhere in it that depth which leads the eye inwards to speculation or relief, the blue that changes with the light. No, this was a sky all self-sufficiency, which could not change or reflect. The tall sharp broken walls reached up into it, and to look at them was to experience their tough hardness, like flakes of old paint magnified. Glittering white were these shards of wall, as the sky was blue, a menacing hardened world.

Emily came into view, her frowning face bent over a task.

She wore a soft blue smock-like garment, like an old-fashioned
child from a nursery, and she held a broom made of twigs, the
kind used in gardens, and she was massing fallen leaves into
heaps that were everywhere on the grass that floored this
broken house. But as she swept, as she made her piles, the leaves
gathered again around her feet. She swept faster, faster, her
face scarlet, desperate. Her broom whirled in a cloud of yellow
and orange leaves. She was trying to empty the house of leaves
so that the wind could not spread them out again. One room
was clear, then another; but outside the leaves lay as high as
her knees: the whole world was thickly covered with the leaves
that descended as fast as snowflakes everywhere from the horrible sky. The world was being submerged in dead leaves,
smothered in them. She turned herself about in an impulsive
movement of panic to see what was happening inside the rooms
she had cleared: already the piles she had made were being
submerged. She ran desperately through the unroofed rooms,
to see if here, or here, or here, would be a place that was still
covered over and sheltered, still safe from the smothering fall
of dead vegetable matter. She did not see me. Her stare, fixed,
wide, horrified, passed over me. She saw only the fragments of
the walls that could not shelter her, nor keep out the sibilant
drift. She stood back against the wall and leaned on her futile
little broom, and looked and listened as the leaves rustled and
fell over and about her and over the whole world in a storm
of decay. She vanished, a staring little figure, a small bright-
coloured girl, like a painted china ornament for a cabinet or a
shelf, a vivid clot of colour on painted whiteness, the horrible
whiteness of the nursery world that opened out of the parents'
bedroom, where the summer or a storm or a snow-world lay
on the other side of thick curtains.

White. White shawls and blankets and bedding and pil-

lows. In an interminable plain of white, an infant lay buried
and unable to free its arms. It stared at a white ceiling. Turning its head, it saw a white wall one way and the edge of a
white cupboard the other. White enamel. White walls. White
wood.

The infant was not alone; something was moving about,
a heavy tramping creature, each footstep making the cot shake.
Thud, thud went the heavy feet, and there was a clash of
metal on stone. The infant lifted its head and could not see;
it strained to hold its head up from the damp heat of the pillow,
but had to let go and fall back into the soft heat. Never—not
until she would come to lie helpless on her deathbed, all
strength gone from her limbs, nothing left to her but the consciousness behind her eyes—would she again be as helpless as
she was now. The enormous tramping creature came thudding
to the cot, whose iron bars shook and rattled, and as the great
face bent over her, she was excavated from the hot white and
whisked up, losing her breath, and was gripped in hands that
pressed on her ribs. She was dirty. Already. Dirty. The sound
of the word was disapproval, disgust, dislike. It meant being
bundled about, turned this way and that, between hard knocking hands, like a piece of filleted fish on a slab, or a chicken
being stuffed.

Dirty, dirty . . . the harsh cold sound of the word, to me
watching this scene, was the air of the "personal," the un-
alterability of the laws of this world. Whiteness, dislike sound-
ing in a word, a frigidity, a smothering, as the air fell and fell,
dragged down by a storm of white in which the puppets jerked
on their strings. . . . *Suppose, then, that the dams were to fill
up with ice and the snows came down for ever, an eternal
descent of white; suppose the rooms filled up with cold powder,
all water gone and crystallised, all warmth held latent in dry*

*chill air that shocked and starved the lungs. . . .* A scene of the
parents' bedroom, where the white curtains are drawn back,
drifts of white dotted muslin: beyond these the snow is white
on white again, for the sky is blotted out. The two great beds—
lifted high, high, halfway to the smothering white ceiling—
are filled. Mother in one, father in the other. There is a new
thing in the room, a cot, all white again, a gelid glittering
white. A tall thing, this cot, not as high as the towering beds
that have the great people in them, but still beyond one's
reach. A white figure bustles in, the one whose bosom is a full
slope, which is hard. A bundle is lifted from the cot. While
the two people in the beds smile encouragingly, this bundle
is held out and presented to her face. The bundle smells, it
smells: sharp and dangerous are these odours, like scissors, or
hard tormenting hands. Such a desolation and an aloneness as
no one in the world (except everyone in the world) has felt,
she feels now, and the violence of her pain is such that she can
do nothing but stand there, stiff, staring first at the bundle,
then at the great white-clothed nurse, then at the mother and
the father smiling in their beds.

She could have sunk down and away from the sight of
them, the smiling ones, the great people held up high there
against the ceiling in their warm stifling room, red and white,
white and red, red carpet, the red flames crowding there in the
fireplace. It is all too much, too high, too large, too powerful; she does not want anything but to creep away and
hide somewhere, to let it all slide away from her. But she is
being presented again and again with the smelling bundle.

"Now, then, Emily, this is your baby," comes the smiling
but peremptory voice from the large woman's bed. "It is your
baby, Emily."

This lie confuses her. Is it a game, a joke at which she

must laugh and protest, as when her father "tickles" her, a torture which will recur in nightmares for years afterwards? Should she now laugh and protest and wriggle? She stares around at the faces, the mother, the father, the nurse, for all have betrayed her. This is not her baby, and they know it, so why . . . But again and again they say, "This is your baby, Emily, and you must love him."

The bundle was being pushed against her, and she was supposed to put her arms out and hold it. Another deception, for she was not holding it; the nurse did. But now they were smiling and commending her for holding the thing in her arms. And so it was all too much, the lies were too much, the love was too much. They were too strong for her. And she did hold the baby: it was always being lifted down to her, against her, towards her. She held it and she loved it with a passionate violent protective love that had at its heart a trick and a betrayal, heat with a core of ice. . . .

Now the room is the one with the red velvet curtains, and a little girl of about four, dressed in a flowered smock, is standing over a pudgy open-mouthed infant who sits slackly on a piece of linoleum stretched across the carpet.

"No, not like that—like this," she commands, as the little boy, gazing in admiration at this strong and clever mentor of his, attempts to put a block on another block. It topples off. "Like *this*," she shrills, and feverishly kneels and puts blocks one on top of another, very fast and skilfully. She is quite absorbed, every atom of her, in her need to do this, to do it well, to show she can do it, to prove to herself she can do it. The amiable infant sits there, is watching, is impressed, but to do it is the thing—yes, to do it, to place the blocks one above the other, perfectly, corner to corner, edge to edge: "No, not like that—like *this!*" The words ring through the room, the room next door, the rooms downstairs, the garden. "Like *this,* Baby, don't you see? Like *this.*"

□  □  □

Things continued to be easier between Emily and me because of my visit to her other home. I was able, for instance, to comment on her smeared face and swollen eyes one morning. She had not been to Gerald's place the day before, and showed no signs of going now. It was already midday and she had not dressed. She wore what she had slept in, a cotton shift-like garment that had once been a summer evening dress. She was on the floor, her arms around Hugo.

"I don't really see what I am doing there at all," she said, and meant it as a question.

"I should have said you were doing everything there."

She held her look steadily on me; she smiled—bitter, and not self-consciously so. "Yes, but if I didn't, someone would."

Now, this I did not expect: it was, if you like, too adult a thought. Even while I was privately commending her on it, I was also reacting with alarm, for the other side of this thought, its shadow, is dark indeed, and leads to every sort of listlessness and despair: it is often the first step, to be precise about it, towards suicide. . . . At the very least, it is the most deadly of the energy-drainers.

But I side-stepped with "Very true. True for every one of us. But that doesn't mean to say we can all stay in bed! But the thought in *my* mind is, why do you feel like this now? This moment. What triggered it off?"

She smiled—oh, yes, she was very quick, very shrewd:
"Well, I'm not going to cut my throat!" And then, in a com-
plete switch of level, a plunge, she cried out, "But if I did,
what of it?"

"Is it Maureen?" I asked. I could think of nothing else
to offer.

My stupidity enabled her to check herself; she was back
again, on her own level. She looked at me; she looked—oh,
those looks, which I took one after another, light mocking
blows. This one meant: *Oh, a melodrama! He does not love
me, he loves another!*

"Maureen . . ." she let slip out of her, like a shrug, and
did in fact shrug. But then, condescending, she allowed: "It is
not Maureen, actually; at this very minute it is June."

And she waited and watched, with her little sour smile,
for my "*What?* Nonsense, it can't be!"

"It's not right, is it?" she mimicked.

"But she's—how old?"

"Actually, she is eleven, but she says she is twelve."

She was smiling now, and out of her own, her real
philosophy: my energetic disapproval was feeding energy into
her, and she even sat up and laughed. My tongue was rejecting,
one after another, an assortment of verbalisations, not one of
which, I knew, could earn anything less than mockery. Finally,
she did mock me again with "Well, she can't get pregnant;
that's something, at least."

I wasn't going to capitulate. "All the same," I said, "it
can't possibly be good for her."

Her smile changed: it was a little sad—envious, perhaps.
It meant: *You forget we are not in a position to afford your
standards. <u>We</u> are not so fortunate—remember?*

Because of this smile, I stayed quiet, and then she said:

"*You're* thinking, Oh, she's just a child, how wrong!—that sort of thing—but *I'm* thinking, June was my friend and now she isn't."

And now I really was silenced. For what nonsense was this? If June was not a friend now, she would be in a week, when Gerald went on to one of the others. In one moment—and it seemed that this happened a dozen times a day—Emily had switched from a realm of sophistication far beyond me (making that word mean an acceptance, an understanding, of how things work) to being a child, really a child, and even as they used to be. . . . I shrugged, leaving her to it. I could not help it; this switchbacking conversation had been too much for me.

Emily felt the shrug as a condemnation of her, and she cried out, "I've never had anyone before—not anyone really close, like June." And her face was turned away to hide a child's tears.

And that is how blind one can be about a thing. For I had been seeing the child June adoring the "older woman," as was natural, and is a stage in every person's growth. I had never understood how much Emily depended on that thin sharp-faced waif, who not only *looked* three years younger but was in a different realm altogether, as different as childhood is from young womanhood.

I could only offer: "You know he will get tired of her and you will be friends again."

She almost shrieked in her exasperation at my old-fashioned ways and thoughts: "It is not a question of getting *tired.*"

"What, then? Tell me."

She looked at me, in her turn shrugged, and said, "Well, things are quite different, aren't they. . . . He just has to—

make the rounds, I suppose. Like a cat marking his territory."
And she laughed, a little, at the thought.

"Well, whatever your original and brilliant new customs
are, the point is, June will be free quite soon, surely?"

"But I miss her *now*," she wept, a little girl again, thumbs
sweeping tears from her eyes; but up she jumped, and said,
as an adult, "Anyway, I have to go there, whether I like it or
not." And off she did go, red-eyed, miserable, full of a suppressed anger that showed in every movement. She went because her sense of duty would not let her do otherwise.

Behind my flowery wall was a straight-upstanding, a tall,
fine, white-shining house. I looked at it from some way off, then
came closer, noting that this was the first time I had approached
a house from outside, instead of finding myself inside another
building from the moment I crossed the mysterious frontier.
It was a solid and well-kept house, in style rather like the
Cape Dutch, whose every sober curve speaks of the burgher,
the bourgeois. The house shone with a peculiar soft glisten. It
was made of a substance which was familiar in itself, but not
when shaped into a house. I broke a piece off it and ate: sweet,
dissolving on the tongue. A sugar house, like the one in fairy
tales; or, if not sugar, then the edible substance they once
used to wrap bars of nougat. I kept breaking off bits and eating
and tasting. . . . It was compulsively edible, because it was un-
satisfying, cloying: one could eat and eat and never be filled
with this white insipidity. There was Emily, breaking off whole
pieces of the roof and cramming them into her healthy
mouth; there, too, was June, languidly picking and choosing.
A fragment of wall, a piece of windowpane . . . we ate and ate
our way into the house like termites, our stomachs laden but
unsatisfied, unable to stop ourselves but nauseated. Eating my
way around a corner, I saw a room in that region I knew

was the "personal." I knew the room. A small room, with strong sunlight coming through the window. A stone floor, and a cot in the middle of it, and in the cot a child, a small girl. Emily, absorbed, oblivious. She was eating—chocolate. No, excrement. She had opened her bowels into the freshness of the white bed and had taken handfuls of the stuff and smeared it everywhere with quick shrieks of triumph and joy. She had smeared it on the sheets and blankets, over the wood of the cot, over herself, over her face, and into her hair, and there she sat, a little monkey, thoughtfully tasting and digesting.

This scene—child, cot, sunlit room—diminished sharply, dwindled in the beam of my vision, and was whisked away to be replaced by the same scene made smaller, reduced by the necessity to diminish and so to contain pain; for suddenly there were heavy clanging steps on the stone, a loud angry voice, slaps, heavy breathing—there were low mutters and then exclamations of disgust, and the child yelling and screaming, first in anger, and then, after an interval when she was half-drowned by the vigor with which she was scrubbed and swished about in a deep and over-hot bath, in despair. She wept in innocent despair as the big woman snuffed and sniffed at her, to see if the stink of shit had been washed away, but found (still, in spite of the too hot water that had scalded and burned, in spite of the scrubbing which had left the fragile skin painful and red) a faint tainted odour, so that she had to keep on exclaiming in disgust and in fright. The mother was exclaiming over and over again in dislike of her; the child was sobbing with exhaustion. She was dumped down in a playpen, and her cot was taken out for a scrubbing and a disinfecting. Alone in her disgrace, she sobbed on and on.

A child crying. The miserable lost sound of incomprehension.

"You are a naughty girl, Emily, naughty, naughty, naughty, disgusting, filthy, dirty, dirty, dirty dirty dirty dirty, a dirty girl, Emily, you are a dirty *naughty*—oh, *disgusting,* you are a filthy dirty dirty girl, Emily."

I wandered looking for her in adjacent rooms, but never finding the right one, though I could hear Emily's misery sometimes very close. Often I knew her to be through a single wall: I could have touched her if there had not been a wall. But, following that wall to its end, it led beyond the "personal," and I was out on a bright green lawn or small field with summer trees standing about its edges. On the lawn was an egg. It was the size of a small house, but poised so lightly that it moved in a breeze. Around this brilliant white egg, under a bright sky, moved Emily, her mother, and her father, and— this was as improbable an association of people as one could conceive—June, too, close to Emily. There they strayed, contented in the sunlight, with the light breeze moving their clothes. They touched the egg. They stood back and looked at it. They smiled; they were altogether full of delight and pleasure. They laid their faces to the smooth healthy slope of the egg's surface, so that their cheeks could experience it; they smelled it; they gently rocked it with their fingertips. All this scene was large and light and pleasurable, was freedom—and from it I turned a corner sharp back to a narrow and dark passageway and the sound of a child's crying. . . . Of course I had been mistaken, she had not been behind *that* wall at all; there was another one, and I knew exactly where it was. I began to run, I ran, I had to reach her. I was conscious that I was also reluctant, for I was not looking forward to the moment when I, too, would smell that faint contaminating smell in her hair, her skin. I was setting myself a task as I ran: I was not to show my repugnance, as her mother had done with her sharply indrawn breath—a controlled retching, the muscles of her stomach convulsing again and again—her quivering dislike of the child communicating itself down through the arms which lifted Emily up and away from the scene of her pleasure, and dropped her sharp and punishing into the bath where the water, from the need for haste, was still cold, but where very hot water was flooding, and the two streams of very hot and very cold water swirled all around her, scalding and freezing her legs and stomach. But I could not find her, I never did find her, and the crying went on and on and on, and I could hear it in the day, in my "real" life.

I've said, I think, that when I was in one world—the region behind the flowery wall of my living-room—the ordinary logical time-dominated world of everyday did not exist; that when I was in my "ordinary" life I forgot, and sometimes for days at a time, that the wall could open, has opened, would open again, and then I would simply move through into that other space. But now began a period when something of the flavour of the place behind the wall did continuously invade my real life. It was manifested at first in the sobbing of a child. Very faint, very distant. Sometimes inaudible, or nearly so, and my ears would strain after it and then lose it. It would begin again, and get quite loud, and even when I was perhaps talking to Emily herself, or standing at the window watching events outside, I heard the sobbing of a child, a child alone, disliked, repudiated; and at the same time, beside it, I could hear the complaint of the mother, the woman's plaint, and the two sounds went on side by side, theme and descant.

I sat listening. I sat by myself and listened. It was warm, over-warm; it was that hot final summer. There was often thunder, sudden dry storms; there was restlessness in the streets, the need to move. . . . I would make little tasks for myself because I had to move. I sat, or kept myself busy, and I listened. One morning Emily came in, all brisk and lively, and, seeing me at work setting plums on trays to dry, she joined me. She was wearing that morning a striped cotton shirt, and jeans. The shirt lacked a button at breast-level, and gaped, showing her already strong breasts. She looked tired, as well as full of energy; she had not yet bathed, and a smell of sex came from her. She was fulfilled and easy, a bit sad, but humorously so. She was, in short, a woman, and she sat smiling, wiping plums with slow easy movements, all the hungers, the drives, and the needs pounded and hunted out of her, exorcised in the recent lovemaking. And all the time that child was crying. I was looking at her; I was thinking, as the elderly do, wrestling with time, the sheer cussedness of the thing—futilely (but they cannot help it)—using the thought over and over again as a kind of measure or guideline: *That was fourteen years ago, less, when you wept so painfully and for so long because of your incomprehension and because of your scalded buttocks and thighs and legs. Fourteen years for me is so short a time, it weighs so light in my scale; in yours, in your scale, it is everything, your whole life.*

She, thinking of time, speaking of it as a girl was once expected to while she marked the slow overtaking of the milestones one by one into womanhood and freedom, said, "I'm coming up to fifteen," because she had just passed her fourteenth birthday. She had said that only yesterday; she was capable of talking like that, even pertly and with a fling of her hair, like a "young girl." Meanwhile she had just come from lovemaking—and no girl's lovemaking, at that.

All that morning, I listened to the sobbing while I sat working with her. But Emily heard nothing, though I couldn't believe it.

"Can't you hear someone crying?" I asked, as casual as could be, while I was twisting and turning inwardly not to hear that miserable sound.

"No, can you?" And off she went to stand at the window, Hugo beside her. She was looking to see if Gerald had arrived yet. He had not. She went to bath, to dress; at the window she stood waiting—yes, there he was; he was just arriving. And now she would stand there a little longer, careful not to see him, so as to assert her independence, to emphasise this other life of hers with me. She would linger here half an hour, an hour. She would even sit down again with her ugly yellow animal, fondling and teasing him. Her silence would grow tense, her stares out of the window more stylised: *Girl at Window Oblivious of Her Lover.* Then her hand on the animal's head, stroking and patting, would forget him, would fall away. Gerald had seen her. He had noticed her *not* noticing him. He had turned away: unlike her, he genuinely did not care very much—or, rather, he did care, but not at all in the same way. At any rate, now, this afternoon, June was there, and Maureen, a dozen other girls. And Emily could not bear it. She went, with a kiss for her Hugo. As for me, I got the ritual "I'll just go out for a little, if that is all right with you."

And in a moment she was with them, her family, her tribe, her life. A striking-looking girl, with her dark hair flat on either side of a pale, too earnest face, she was where Gerald was, who swaggered there with the knives in his belt, his whiskers, his strong brown arms. Good Lord, how many centuries had we overturned, how many long slow steps of man's upclimbing did Emily undo when she crossed from my flat to the life on the pavement! And what promise, what possibilities, what experiments, what variations on the human theme had been cancelled out! Watching, I fell into despair at

the precariousness of every human attempt and effort, and I
left the window. It was that afternoon I tried deliberately to
reach behind the wall: I stood there a long time looking and
waiting. The wall did not have light lying on it now, was
uniform, dull, blank. I went up and pressed my palms against
it, and moved my hands all over it, feeling and sensing, trying
everything to make the heavy solidity of the thing go down
under the pressure of my will. It was nonsense, I knew that;
it was never because of my, or anybody's, wanting when that
wall went down and made a bridge or a door. But the interminable low sobbing, the miserable child, was driving me
frantic, was depriving me of ordinary sense. . . . Yet by turning
my head I could see her: a lusty young girl on the pavement—
unsmiling, perhaps, because of her innate seriousness, but very
far indeed from weeping. It was the child I wanted to pick
up and kiss and soothe. And the child was so close, it was a
question only of finding the right place on the wall to press,
as in the old stories. A particular flower in the pattern, or a
point found by counting just so many inches from here to there
and then gently pushed . . . but, of course, I knew there could
be nothing in a deliberate attempt of the will. Yet I stood there
all afternoon, and into the evening as it darkened outside and
the flares were lit on the pavement, showing the crowding
masses eating, drinking, milling about in their clans and alliances. I let my palms move over to the wall, slowly, inch by
inch, but I did not find a way in that day, nor the next; I never
did find that weeping child who remained there, sobbing
hopelessly alone and disowned, and with long years in front
of her to live through before time could put strength into her
and set her free.

    I never found Emily. But I did find . . . the thing is, what
I did find was inevitable. I could have foreseen it. The finding

had about it, had in it as its quintessence, the banality, the
tedium, the smallness, the restriction of that "personal" dimension. What else could I find—unexpectedly, it goes without
saying—when behind that wall I ran and ran along passages,
along corridors, into rooms where I *knew* she must be but
where she was not, until at last I found her: a blond blue-eyed
child, but the blue eyes were reddened and sullen with weeping. Who else could it possibly be but Emily's mother, the large
cart-horse woman, her tormentor, the world's image? It was
not Emily I took up in my arms, and whose weeping I tried
to shush. Up went the little arms, desperate for comfort, but
they would be one day those great arms that had never been
taught tenderness; the face, scarlet with need, was solaced at
last into a pain-drained exhaustion as the fair little child collapsed, head on my shoulder, and the soft wisps of gold baby-
hair came up dry and pretty as I rubbed the dank strands
gently through my fingers to absorb the sweat. A pretty, fair
little girl, at last finding comfort in my arms . . . and who was
it I saw at an earlier stage than the scene where a little girl
joyously smeared the chocolate-brown faeces into her hair, her
face, her bedding? For once, following a low sobbing, I walked
into a room that was all white and clean and sterile, the nightmare colour of Emily's deprivation. A nursery. Whose? This
was before a brother or sister had been born, for she was tiny,
a baby, and alone. The mother was elsewhere; it was not time
to feed. The baby was desperate with hunger. Need clawed
in her belly; she was being eaten alive by the need for food.
She yelled inside the thick smothering warmth; sweat scattered
off her scarlet little face; she twisted her head to find a breast,
a bottle, anything; she wanted liquid, warmth, food, comfort.
She twisted and fought and screamed. And screamed—for
time must pass before she was fed, the strict order of the regime

said it must be so: nothing could move that obdurate woman there, who had set her own needs and her relation with her baby according to some timetable alien to them both, and who would obey it to the end. I knew I was seeing an incident that was repeated again and again in Emily's? her mother's? early life. It was a continuing thing; had gone on, day after day, month after month. There had been a screaming and hungry—then a whimpering and sullen—baby, wanting the next meal, which did not come or, if it did come, was not enough. There was something in that strong impervious woman which made this so, dictated it. Necessity. The strict laws of this small personal world. Heat. Hunger. A fighting of emotion. The hot red running of flames from a barred fireplace on white walls, white wool, white wood, white, white. The smell of sick rising from the wet that grated under the chin, the smell of wet heavy wool. And smallness, extreme smallness, weakness, a helplessness reaching out and crying for the little crumbs of food, freedom, variation of choice which were all that could reach this little hot place where the puppets jerk to their invisible strings.

□   □   □

I think this is the right place to say something more about "it." Though of course there is no "right" place or time, since there was no particular moment that marked "its" beginning. And yet there did come a period when everyone was talking about "it"; and we knew we had not been doing this until recently: there was a different ingredient in our lives.

Perhaps it might even have been more correct to have

begun this chronicle with an attempt at a full description of "it." But is it possible to write an account of anything at all without "it"—in some shape or another—being the main theme? Perhaps, indeed, "it" is the secret theme of all literature and history, like writing between the lines in invisible ink, which springs up, sharply black, dimming the old print we knew so well, as life, personal or public, unfolds unexpectedly and we see something where we never thought we could—we see "it" as the ground-swell of events, experience. . . . Very well, then, but what *was* "it"? . . . I am sure that ever since there were men on earth, "it" has been talked of precisely in this way in times of crisis, since it is in crisis "it" becomes visible, and our conceit sinks before its force. For "it" is a force, a power, taking the form of earthquake, a visiting comet whose balefulness hangs closer night by night, distorting all thought by fear—"it" can be, has been, pestilence, a war, the alteration of climate, a tyranny that twists men's minds, the savagery of a religion.

"It," in short, is the word for helpless ignorance, or of helpless awareness. "It" is a word for man's inadequacy?

*"Have you heard anything new about it?"*

*"So-and-so said last that it . . ."*

Worse still when the stage is reached of "Have you heard anything new?" when "it" has absorbed everything into itself, and nothing else can be meant when people ask what is moving in our world, what moves our world. "It." Only "it," a much worse word than "they"; for "they" at least are humanity, too, can be moved, are helpless, like ourselves.

"It," perhaps—on this occasion in history—was, above all, a consciousness of something ending.

How would Emily put what she felt into words? She would describe this, perhaps, in terms of that image of her

sweeping, sweeping—the sorcerer's apprentice put to work in a
spiteful garden against floods of dying leaves that she could
never clean away no matter how hard she tried. Her sense of
duty but expressed in images: she could not say of herself that
yes, she was a good little girl and not a bad dirty little girl;
a good little girl who must love, cherish, and protect her
brother, her baby, the defenceless, the powerless, the amiably
indifferently smiling, who sat there all loose and slack in their
damp strong-smelling white wool. "It was so hard," she might
say. "Everything was so difficult, such an effort, such a burden,
all those children in the house, not one of them would do a
thing to help unless I got at them all the time, they turned me
into a tyrant and laughed at me, but there was no need for
that, they could have had something equal and easy if they
had done their parts but no, I always had to overlook everything, comb their dirty hair and see if they had washed, and
then all those sores that they got when they wouldn't eat sensibly, and the horrible smell of disinfectants all the time that
the government supplied and the way June got sick, it drove
me crazy with worry, she kept getting ill for no particular
reason—that was it, there was never any good reason for
things, and I worked and I worked and it was always the
same, something happened and then it all came to nothing."

Yes, that is probably how Emily's version of that time
would sound.

June, returning with Emily to my flat one day, about a
fortnight after her induction into womanhood—I put it like
that because this was how she obviously felt it—had changed
physically, and in every way. Her experience had marked her
face, which was even more defenceless, in her sad-waif style,
than before. And she was looking older than Emily. Her body
still had the flat thickness through the waist of a child, and her

breasts had fattened without shaping. Anxiety, or love, had made her eat enough to put on weight. We saw her, that eleven-year-old, as she would look as a middle-aged woman: the thick working body, the face that accommodated, that always seemed able to accommodate, two opposing qualities— the victim's patient helplessness, the sharp inquisitiveness of the user.

June was not well. Our questions brought out of her that this was nothing new; she hadn't been too good "for quite a time." Symptoms? "I dunno, jst feel bad, you know what I mean."

She had stomach pains and frequent headaches. She lacked energy—but energy cannot be expected of a Ryan. She "jst didn't feel good anywhere at all—it comes and goes, reely."

This affliction was not only June's; it was known to a good many of us.

Vague aches and pains; indispositions that came and went, but not according to the terms and times prescribed by the physicians; infections that seemed to be from a common source, since they would go through the community like an epidemic, but not with an epidemic's uniformity—they demonstrated their presence in different symptoms with every victim; rashes that did not seem to have any cause; nervous diseases that could end in bouts of insanity or produce tics or paralyses; tumours and skin diseases; aches and pains that "wandered" about the body; new diseases altogether that for a time were categorised with the old ones for lack of information, until it became clear that these *were* new diseases; mysterious deaths; exhaustions and listlessness that kept people lying about or in bed for weeks and caused relatives and even themselves to use the words "malinger" and "neurotic," and so on, but then, suddenly vanishing, released the poor sufferers from criticism and self-doubt.

In short, there had been for a long time a general increase in illness, both traditional and newly evolved, and if June complained of "just not feeling good anywhere, do you see what I mean?"—then we did, for it was common enough to be classed as a recognisable illness in itself. June decided to move in with us, "for a few days," she said, but what she needed was to evade the pressures, psychological or otherwise, of Gerald's household, and Emily and I knew, if June did not, that she would have liked to leave there altogether.

I offered the big sofa in the living-room to June, but she preferred a mattress on Emily's floor, and even, I think, slept on it, though of course I wondered. Silently wondered. Too often had I experienced a sharp shocked reaction to questions asked innocently. I really did not know if Emily and June would consider lesbianism as the most normal thing in the world, or as improper. Styles in morals had changed so sharply and so often in my lifetime, and were so different in various sections of the community, that I had learned long ago to accept whatever was the norm for that particular time and place. I rather believe that the two girls slept in each other's arms for comfort. Of course I could have no doubt, after what Emily had told me, about how she must feel now she had the child, her "real friend," alone with her there. Almost alone— there was me and there was Hugo. But at least there weren't so many others around all the time.

Emily tried to "nurse" June; that is to say, she fussed and offered food. But a Ryan doesn't eat like an ordinary citizen: June nibbled, all fancies and antipathies. Probably she was, as Emily said, suffering from vitamin deficiencies, but she said, "That doesn't make sense to my mind: I never eat any different, do I? But I feel bad inside and everywhere now, don't I, and I didn't before."

So if June were asked to say what "it" was like for her, she would very likely answer, "Well, I dunno, reely; I feel bad inside and everywhere."

Perhaps, after all, one has to end by characterising "it" as a sort of cloud or emanation, but invisible, like the water vapour you know is present in the air of the room you sit in, makes part of the air you know is there when you look out of a window; your eye is traversing air, so your intellect tells you when you look at a sparrow pecking insects off a twig, and you know that the air is part water vapour which at any moment—as a slap of cold air comes in from somewhere else—will condense as mist or fall as rain. "It" was everywhere, in everything, moved in our blood, our minds. "It" was nothing that could be described once and for all, or pinned down, or kept stationary; "it" was an illness, a tiredness, boils; "it" was the pain of watching Emily, a fourteen-year-old girl, locked inside her necessity to—sweep away dead leaves; "it" was the price or unreliability of the electricity supply; the way telephones didn't work; the migrating tribes of cannibals; was "them" and their antics; "it" was, finally, what you experienced . . . and was in the space behind the wall, moved the players behind the wall, just as much there as in our ordinary world, where one hour followed another and life obeyed the unities, like a certain kind of play.

As that summer ended, there was as bad a state of affairs in the space behind the wall as on this side, with us. Or perhaps it was only that I was seeing what went on there more clearly. Instead of entering into a room, or a passageway, where there was a door which opened into other rooms and passages, so that I was within a sense of opportunities and possibilities, but limited always to the next turn of the corridor, the opening of the next door—the sense of plenty, of space always opening

out and away kept within a framework of order, within which
I was placed as part of it—now it seemed as if a perspective
had shifted and I was seeing the sets of rooms from above, or
as if I were able to move through them so fast I could visit
them all at once and exhaust them. At any rate, the feeling of
surprise, of expectancy, had gone, and I could even say that
these sets and suites of rooms, until so recently full of alternatives and possibilities, had absorbed into them something of the
claustrophobic air of the realm of the "personal," with its rigid
necessities. And yet the disorder there had never been so great.
Sometimes it seemed to me as if all those rooms had been set
up, carefully, correct to the last detail, simply in order to be
knocked flat again, as if a vast house had been taken over and
decorated to display a hundred different manners, modes,
epochs—but quite arbitrarily, not consecutively and in order to
give a sense of the growth of one style into another. Set up,
perfected—and then knocked flat.

I cannot begin to give an idea of the mess in those rooms.
Perhaps I could not go into a room at all, it was so heaped with
cracking and splintering furniture. Other rooms had been used,
or so they looked, as refuse dumps: stinking piles of rubbish
filled them. Some had their furniture neatly set out in them,
but the roofs had gone, or the walls gaped. Once I saw in the
centre of a formal and rich room—French, Second Empire, as
lifeless as if it had been arranged for a museum—the remains
of a fire built on a piece of old iron, some sleeping bags left
anyhow, a big pot full of cold boiled potatoes near the wall in
line with a dozen pairs of boots. I knew the soldiers would
come back suddenly, and if I wanted to keep my life I should
leave. Already there was a corpse, with dried blood staining the
carpet around it.

And yet, with all these evidences of destructiveness, even

now I could not move behind the wall without feeling something of the old expectation, hope, even longing. And rightly, for when the anarchy was at its height, and I had almost lost the habit of expecting anything but smashed and dirtied rooms, there was a visit when I found this: I was in a garden between four walls, old brick walls, and there was a fresh delightful sky above me that I knew was the sky of another world, not ours. This garden did have a few flowers in it, but mostly it had vegetables. There were beds neatly filled with greenery— carrot tops, lettuces, radishes, and there were tomatoes, and gooseberry bushes, and ripening melons. Some beds were raked and ready for planting; others had been turned and left open to the sun and the air. It was a place filled with industry, usefulness, hope. I walked there under a fruitful sky, and thought of how people would be fed from this garden. But this wasn't all, for I became aware that under this garden was another. I was able easily to make my way down into it along a sloping ramp of earth, and there were even steps of—I think —stone. I was down in the lower garden, which was immediately under the first and occupied the same area: the feeling of comfort and security this gave me is really not describable. Nor was this lower garden any less supplied with sun, wind, rain than the upper one. Here, too, were the tall warm walls of weathered brick, and the beds in various stages of preparedness and use. There was an exquisite old rose growing on one wall. It was a soft yellow, and its scent was in all the air of the garden. Some pinks and mignonette grew near a sunny stone: these were the old flowers, rather small, but subtle and individual: all the old cottage flowers were here, among the leeks and the garlics and the mints. There was a gardener. I saw him at the moment I realised I was listening with pleasure to the sound of water running near my feet, where there was a chan-

nel of earth, with tiny herbs and grasses growing along its
edges. Near the wall the channel was of stone, and wider: the
gardener was bending over the stone runnel where it came
into the garden from outside through a low opening that was
green and soft with moss. Around every bed was a stream of
clear water; the garden was a network of water channels. And,
looking up and beyond the wall, I saw that the water came
from the mountains four or five miles away. There was snow
on them, although it was midsummer, and this was melted
snow-water, very cold, and tasting of the air that blew across
the mountains. The gardener turned when I ran towards him
to ask if he had news of the person whose presence was so
strong in this place, as pervasive as the rose-scent, but he only
nodded and turned back to his duties of controlling the flow
of water, of seeing that it ran equably among the beds. I
looked across at the mountains and at the plain between,
where there were villages and large stone houses in gardens,
and I thought that what I was looking at was the under-
world—and one just as extensive and productive—of the level
to which I now had to return. I walked up to the first level
again, and saw the old walls warm with evening sunlight,
heard water running everywhere, though I had not heard it
when I stood here before; I took small cautious steps from one
solid but moist spot to the next, with the smell of apple-mint
coming up from my knees and the sound of bees in my ears.
I looked at the food the earth was making, which would keep
the next winter safe for us, for the world's people. Gardens
beneath gardens, gardens above gardens: the food-giving sur-
faces of the earth doubled, trebled, endless—the plenty of it,
the richness, the generosity . . .

And back in my ordinary life, I watched June listless in
a deep chair, shaking her head with a patient smile at a plate
of food being held towards her by Emily.

"But she has to eat, hasn't she?" said Emily to me, sharp with worry, and when the child continued to smile and refuse, Emily whirled about and set the plate down in front of Hugo, who, knowing he was being used to demonstrate rejection, as if she were tipping food into a rubbish bin, turned his face away. I saw Emily then, all loving remorse, sit by her neglected slave, and put her face down into his fur, as once she had so often been used to do. I saw how he turned his head a little towards her, despite his intention not to show response, let alone pleasure. Despite himself, he licked her hand a little, with a look on him that a person has when doing something he doesn't want to do, but can't stop . . . and she sat there and wept, she wept. There they were, the three of them, June with her malady, whatever it was, the ugly yellow beast in his humility, suffering his heartache, and the fierce young woman. I sat quiet among the three of them, and thought of the gardens that lay one above another so close to us, behind a wall which at this time of the day—it was evening—lay quite blank and with no depth in it, no promise. I thought of what riches there were in store for these creatures and all the others like them; and though it was hard to maintain a knowledge of that other world, with its scents and running waters and its many plants, while I sat here in this dull shabby daytime room —the pavement outside seething as usual with its tribal life— I did hold it. I kept it in my mind. I was able to do this. Yes, towards the end it was so; intimations of that life, or lives, became more powerful and frequent in "ordinary" life, as if that place were feeding and sustaining us, and wished us to know it. A wind blew from one place to the other; the air of one place was the air of the other; as I came to the window after an escape into the space behind the wall, there would be a moment of doubt; my mind would sway and have to steady itself as I reassured myself that no, what I was looking at was reality, was real life; I was standing foursquare in what every-body would concur was normality.

□   □   □

By the end of that summer there were hundreds of peo-ple of all ages on the pavement. Gerald was now only one of a dozen or so leaders. Among them was a middle-aged man—a new development, this. There was also a woman, who led a small band of girls. They were self-consciously and loudly critical of male authority, male organisation, as if they had set themselves a duty always to be there commenting on everything the men did. They were a chorus of condemnation. Yet the leader seemed to find it necessary to spend a great deal of energy preventing individuals of her flock from straying off and attaching themselves to the men. This caused a good deal of not always good-natured comment from the men, some-times from the other women. But the problems and difficulties everyone had to face made this kind of disagreement seem minor. And it was an efficient group, showing great tenderness to each other and to children, always ready with information—still the most important of the commodities—and generous with what food and goods they had.

It was to the women's group that we lost June.

It happened like this. Emily had again taken to spend-ing most of her days and nights at the other house: duty had taken her back, for messages had come that she was needed. She wanted June to move with her, and June did listen to Emily's persuasions, agreed with her—but did not go. I began to think that I was to lose Emily, my real charge, for June, and

I did not feel any particular responsibility for her. I liked
the child, though her listless presence lowered the atmosphere
of my home, making me listless, too, and keeping Hugo in a
permanent sorrow of jealousy. I was pleased enough when
she roused herself to talk to me: for the most part she lay in a
corner of the sofa, doing nothing at all. But the truth was I
would have liked her to leave. She asked after Gerald when
Emily came flying home to cook a meal of her favourite chips,
to make pots of precious tea, to serve her cups half filled with
precious sugar: she listened, and asked after this and that
person; she liked to gossip. She said to me, to Emily, and
doubtless to herself, that she was going—yes, she would go
tomorrow. She confronted Emily's frenzies of anxiety with
"I'll come over tomorrow—yes, I will, Emily," but she stayed
where she was.

On the pavement Emily was being very energetic. Gerald's
troop was about fifty strong, with the people actually living
in his household and the others who had gravitated towards
him from the crowds who kept coming in, and in, during the
long hot afternoons.

Emily was always to be seen near Gerald, prominent in
her role of adviser, source of information. I now did what I
had once been careful to avoid, for fear of upsetting Emily, of
disturbing some balance. I crossed the street myself "to see
what was going on"—as if I had not been watching what went
on for so many months! But this was how all the older citizens
described their first, or indeed their subsequent trips to the
pavement—described them often right up to the moment when
they put together a blanket, some warm clothes, and a little
food to leave the city with a tribe passing through, or one
taking off from our pavement. I even wondered if perhaps
this visit of mine away from my flat to across the street was a

sign of an inner intention to leave which I knew nothing about
yet. This was so attractive an idea that as soon as it had entered
my head, it took possession and I had to fight it down. My
first trip to the pavement—to stand there, to mill around with
the others for an hour or so—was really to hear what it was that
Emily so ably, and for so many hours every day, dispensed
out there. Well, I was astounded. . . . How often had this girl
taken me by surprise! Now I drifted around among this restless, lively, ruthless crowd and saw how everyone, not only
those who seemed ready to owe allegiance to Gerald, turned
to her for news, information, advice. And she was ready
with it. Yes, there were dried apples in such-and-such a shop
in that suburb. No, the bus for a village twenty miles west was
not cancelled altogether: it still ran once a week until Decem-
ber, and there was a trip next Monday at 10 a.m., but you
would have to be there in the queue the night before and must
be prepared to fight for your place; it would be worth it, for
it was said there were plentiful supplies of apples and plums.
A farmer was coming in by cart every Friday with mutton fat
and hides, and could be found at . . . Big strong horses were for
sale or barter. And yes, there was a house four streets away
quite suitable for stabling. As for fodder, that could be pro-
cured, but better still, grow it, and for one horse you would
need . . . A variety of chemical devices for cooking and lighting
were being constructed tomorrow afternoon on the second
floor of the old Plaza Hotel; assistance was needed and would
be paid for in the form of the said devices. Wood ash, horse
manure, compost would be for sale under the old motorway
at Smith Street at 3 p.m. on Sunday. Lessons in making your
own wind-generators, to be paid for in food and fuel . . . Air
cleansers and purifiers, water cleansers, earth sterilisers . . .
laying fowls and coops for them . . . knife-sharpeners . . . A

man who knew the plan of the underground sewers and the rivers that ran into them was piping water to the surface at . . . The street between X Road and Y Crescent was growing superb crops of yarrow and coltsfoot, and on the corner of Piltdown Way was a patch of potatoes people had planted and then forgotten: they had probably left the city. Emily knew all these things and many more, and was much sought after by virtue of her energy and her equipment in that scene like a fair where hundreds of egos clashed and competed and fed each other—Emily, Gerald's girl. So she was referred to, so spoken of. This surprised me, knowing the state of affairs in that house I had visited. This was yet another emotional, or at least verbal, hangover from the past? A man had a woman, an official woman, like a first wife, even when he virtually ran a harem? . . . if one could use one old-fashioned term, then why not another? I did try the word out on June: "Gerald's harem," I said; and her little face puzzled up at me. She had heard the word, but had not associated it with anything that could come close to her. But yes, she had seen a film; and yes, Gerald had a harem. She, June, was part of it. She even giggled, looking at me with those pale blue eyes that seemed always to be swallowing astonishment. There she lay, seeing herself as a harem girl, a little ageing woman, with her childish flat waist, her child's eyes, her pale hair dragged to one side.

Emily of course had marked my appearance on the pavement, and was assuming I was ready to migrate. And how attractive it was there with those masses of vigorous people, all so resourceful in the ways of this hand-to-mouth world, so easy and inventive in everything they did. What a relief it would be to throw off, in one movement like a shrug of the shoulders, all the old ways, the old problems—these, once one took a step across the street to join the tribes, would dissolve, lose importance. Housekeeping now could be just as accurately described as cavekeeping, and was such a piddling, fiddly business. The shell of one's life was a setting for "every modern convenience," but inside the shell one bartered and captured and even stole; one burned candles and huddled over fires made of wood split with an axe. And these people, these tribes, were going to turn their backs on it all and simply take to the roads. Yes, of course they would have to stop somewhere, find an empty village, and take it over; or settle where the farmers that survived would let them, in return for their labour or for acting as private armies. They would have to make for themselves some sort of order again, even if it was no more than that appropriate to outlaws living in and off a forest in the north. Responsibilities and duties there would have to be, and would harden and stultify, probably very soon. But in the meantime, for weeks, months, perhaps with luck even a year or so, an earlier life of mankind would rule: disciplined, but democratic (when these people were at their best, even a child's voice was listened to with respect); all property worries gone; all sexual taboos gone (except for the new ones, but new ones are always more bearable than the old); all problems shared and carried in common. Free. Free, at least from what was left of "civilisation" and its burdens. Infinitely enviable, infinitely desirable, and how I longed simply to close my home up and go. But how could I? There was Emily. As long as she stayed, I would. I began again to talk tentatively of the Dolgellys, of how we would ask for a shed there and build it up and make it into a home—June as well, of course. For from the frantic anxiety Emily showed, I could see it would not be possible for Emily to be separated from June.

And Hugo? The truth is she did not have time for him,

and I was thinking that if he had been what kept her here before, this was not true now.

I believe that he gave up hope altogether during that time when Emily was hardly ever with us and only flew in to see June. One day I saw him sitting openly at the window, all of his ugly stubbornly yellow self visible to anyone who chose to look. It was a challenge, or indifference. He was seen, of course. Some youngsters crossed the street to look at the yellow animal sitting there, gazing steadily back at them with his cat's eyes. It occurred to me that some of the youngest there, the real children of five or six years old, might never have seen a cat or a dog as a "pet" to love and make part of a family.

"Oh, he is ugly," I heard, and saw the children make faces and drift off. No, there would be nothing to help Hugo when the time came for him; no one could say, "Oh, don't kill him; he's such a handsome beast."

Well . . . Emily came in one evening and saw the blaze of yellow at the window. Hugo was vividly there, illuminated by a flare from the late sunset, and by the candles. She was shocked, knowing at once why he should have chosen to disobey the instincts of self-protection.

"Hugo," she said. "Oh, my dear Hugo . . ." He kept his back to her, even when she put her hands on either side of his neck and brought her face down into his fur. He would not soften, and she knew he was saying that she had given him up, and did not care for him.

She coaxed him off the high seat and sat with him on the floor. She began to cry, an irritable, irritating, sniffing sort of weeping that was from exhaustion. I could see that. So could June, who watched without moving. And so could Hugo. He licked her hand at last and lay himself patiently down, saying to her by the way he did this: *It is to please you. I don't care to live if you don't care for me.*

Now Emily was all conflict, all anxiety. She kept rushing back and forth from my flat to that house, between there and the pavement. June, she had to see June, to bring her the bits of food she liked, to make the gesture of getting her into bed at a decent hour, for, left to herself, June would be in that sofa corner until four or six in the morning, doing nothing, except perhaps to mark the interior movements of her illness, whatever that might be. And Hugo, she had to make a point of fussing over Hugo, of loving him. It was as if she had set herself the duty of paying attention to Hugo, measured, like a medicine or a food. And there was myself, the dry old guardian, the mentor—a pull of some sort, I suppose. There were the children, always sending after her if she stayed away from that house for too long. She was worn out; she was cross and sharp and harried and it was a misery to see her at it.

And then, suddenly, it was all over.

It was solved: June left.

She got herself out of the sofa one day and was on the pavement again. Why? I don't know. I never knew what moved June. At any rate, in the afternoons she was again with the crowds out there. She did not seem to be more part of one group than another: her flat, pale, effaced little person was to be seen as much in the other clans as in the one that Gerald held together. She was seen, but only once or twice, in the women's group. And then the women's group had gone and June had gone with them.

And yes, we did not believe it; did not even, at first, know what had happened. June was not in my flat. She was not on the pavement. She was not in that other house. Emily ran frantically about, asking questions. At that point she was stunned. June had left, just like that, without even leaving a message? Yes, that's what it looked like: she had been heard to say, so someone reported, that she felt like moving on.

It was this business of June's not having said goodbye, or not leaving a message, that Emily could not swallow. June had not given any indication at all? We talked it over, the crumbs we had between us, and at last we were able to offer to the situation the fact that June had said on the day she left, "Well, ta, I'll be seeing you around, I expect." But she had not directed this particularly to Emily, or to me. How could we have understood this was her farewell before going away for good?

It was the inconsequence of the act that shocked. June did not believe we were worth the effort of saying goodbye? She had not said a real goodbye because she thought we would stop her? No, we could not believe that was it: she would have stayed as readily as she had left. The shocking truth was that June did not feel *she* was worth the effort: her leaving us, she must have felt, was of no importance. In spite of the fact that Emily was so devoted, and anxious and loving? Yes, in spite of that. June did not value herself. Love, devotion, effort could only pour into her, a jug without a bottom, and then pour out, leaving no trace. She deserved nothing, was owed nothing, could not really be loved, and therefore could not be missed. So she had gone. Probably one of the women had been kind to her, and to this little glow of affection June had responded, as she had to Emily's. She had gone because she could leave one day as well as another. It did not matter, she did not matter. At last we agreed that the energetic and virile woman who led that band had captured the listless June with her energy, at a time when Emily did not have enough to go around.

Emily could not take it in.

And then she began to cry. At first the violent shocked tears, the working face and blank staring eyes of a child, which express only *What, is this happening to me! It's impossible! It isn't fair!* Floods of tears, noisy sobs, exclamations of anger and disgust, but all the time the as it were painted eyes untouched: *Me, it is me sitting here, to whom this frightful injustice has occurred.* . . . A great fuss and a noise and a crying out, this kind of tears, but hardly intolerable, not painful, not a woman's tears . . .

Which came next.

Emily, eyes shut, her hands on her thighs, rocked herself back and forth and from side to side, and she was weeping as a woman weeps, which is to say as if the earth were bleeding. I nearly said, "as if the earth had decided to have a good cry," but it would be dishonest to take the edge off it. Listening, I certainly would not have been able to do less than pay homage to the rock-bottom quality of the act of crying as a grown woman cries.

Who else can cry like that? Not an old woman. The tears of old age can be miserable, can be abject, as bad as anything you like. But they are tears that know better than to demand justice, they have learned too much, they do not have that abysmal quality as of blood ebbing away. A small child can cry as if all the lonely misery of the universe is his alone—it is not the pain in a woman's crying that is the point; no, it is finality of the acceptance of a wrong. So it was, is now, and must ever be, say those closed oozing eyes, the rocking body, the grief. Grief—yes, an act of mourning; that's it. Some enemy has been faced, has been tackled, but a battle has been lost, all the chips are down, everything is spent, nothing is left, nothing can be expected. . . . Yes, in spite of myself, every word I put down is on the edge of farce; somewhere there is a yell of laughter—just as there is when a woman cries in precisely that way. For in life there is often a yell of laughter, which is every bit as intolerable as the tears. I sat there, I went on sitting, watching Emily the eternal woman at her task of weeping. I wished I could go away, knowing it would make no difference to her whether I was there or not. I would have liked to give her something: comfort, friendly arms—a nice cup of tea? (Which in due time I would offer.) No, I had to listen. To grief, to the expression of the intolerable. What on earth, the observer has to ask—husband, lover, mother, friend, even someone who has at some point wept those tears herself, but particularly, of course, husband or lover—"What in the name of God can you possibly have expected of me, of life, that you can now cry like that? Can't you see that it is impossible, *you* are impossible, *no one* could ever have been promised enough to make such tears even feasible . . . can't you see that?" But it is no use. The blinded eyes stare through you; they are seeing some ancient enemy which is, thank heavens, not yourself. No, it is Life or Fate or Destiny, some such force which has struck that woman to the heart, and for ever will she sit, rocking in her grief, which is archaic and dreadful, and the sobs which are being torn out of her are one of the pillars on which everything has to rest. Nothing less could justify them.

In due course, Emily keeled over, lay in a huddle on the floor, and, the ritual subsiding into another key altogether, she snuffled and hiccupped like a child and finally went to sleep.

But when she woke up she did not go back to the other house, she did not go out to the pavement. There she sat, coming to terms. And there she would have stayed for good, very likely, if she had not been challenged.

Gerald came over to see her. Yes, he had been in before, and often for advice. Because his coming was nothing new, we did not know that his problem, our problem, was anything new. And he didn't, at this stage.

He wanted to talk about "a gang of new kids" for whom he felt a responsibility. They were living in the Underground, coming up in forays for food and supplies. Nothing new about that, either. A lot of people had taken to a subterranean existence, though they were felt to be a bit odd, with so many empty homes and hotels. But they could be actively wanted by the police, or criminal in some way, feeling the Underground to be safer.

These "kids," then, were living like moles or rats in the earth, and Gerald felt he should do something about it, and he wanted Emily's support and help. He was desperate for her to rouse herself, and to energise him with her belief and her competence.

He was all appeal; Emily all listlessness and distance. The situation was comic enough. Emily, a woman, was sitting there expressing with every bit of her the dry You want me back, you need me—look at you, a suitor, practically on your knees, but when you have me you don't value me; you take me for granted. *And what about the others?* Irony inspired her pose and gestures, set a gleam of intelligence that was wholly critical on her eyelids. On his side he knew he was being reproached, and that he certainly must be guilty of something or other, but he had had no idea until this moment of how deeply she felt it, how great his crime must be. He confronted her, searching his memory for behaviour which at the time he had committed it he had felt as delinquent, and which he could see now—if he really tried, and he *was* prepared to try—as faulty . . . is this, perhaps, the primal comic situation?

He stuck it out. So did she. He was like a boy in his torn

jersey and worn jeans. A very young man indeed was this
brigand, the young chieftain. He looked tired, he looked anxious; he looked as if he needed to put his head on someone's
shoulder and be told, "There, there!" He looked as if he needed
a good feed and to have his sleep out for once. Is there any
need to describe what happened? Emily smiled at last, dryly,
and for herself (for *he* could not see why she smiled, and she
would not be disloyal to him in sharing it with me); she roused
herself in response to the appeal which he had no idea he was
making, the real one, for he went on logically explaining and
exhorting. In a short time they were discussing the problems
of their household like two young parents. Then off she went
with him, and for some days I did not see her, and only by
fits and starts did I come to understand the nature of this
new problem, and what was so difficult about these particular
"kids." Not only from Emily did I learn: when I joined the
people on the pavement, everybody was talking about them;
they were everyone's problem.

A new one. In understanding why this was, we house-
holders had to come to terms with how far we had travelled
from that state when we swapped tales and rumours about
"those people out there," about the migrating tribes and gangs.
Once, and only a short time ago, to watch—and fearfully—a
mob go past our windows was the limit of our descent into
anarchy. Once, a few months ago, we had seen these gangs
as altogether outside any kind of order. Now we wondered
if and when we should join them. But, above all, the point
was that when studied, when understood, their packs and
tribes had structure, like those of primitive man or of animals,
where in fact a strict order prevails. A short time with people
living this sort of life and one grasped the rules—all unwritten,
of course, but one knew what to expect.

And this was precisely where these new children were differ-

ent. No one knew what to expect. Before, the numerous children without parents attached themselves willingly to families
or to other clans or tribes. They were wild and difficult,
problematical, heartbreaking; they were not like the children
of a stable society, but they could be handled inside the terms
of what was known and understood.

Not so this new gang of "kids." Gangs, rather: soon we
learned that there were others; it was not only in our district that such packs of very young children defied all attempts
at assimilation. For they were very young. The oldest were
nine, ten. They seemed never to have had parents, never to
have known the softening of the family. Some had been born
in the Underground and abandoned. How had they survived?
No one knew. But this is what these children knew how to do.
They stole what they needed to live on, which was very little
indeed. They wore clothes—just enough. They were . . . no,
they were *not* like animals who have been licked and purred
over, and, like people, have found their way to good behaviour
by watching exemplars. They were not a pack, either, but an
assortment of individuals together only for the sake of the
protection in numbers. They had no loyalty to each other, or,
if so, a fitful and unpredictable loyalty. They would be hunting
in a group one hour, and murdering one of their number the
next. They ganged up on each other according to the impulse
of the moment. There were no friendships among them, only
minute-by-minute alliances, and they seemed to have no memory of what had happened even minutes before. There were
thirty or forty in the pack in our neighbourhood, and for the
first time I saw people showing the uncontrolled reactions of
real panic. They were going to call the police, the army; they
would have the children smoked out of the Underground. . . .

A woman from the building I lived in had gone out

with some food to see "if anything could be done for them," and had met a couple on a foray. She had offered them food, which they had eaten then and there, tearing it and snapping and snarling at each other. She had waited, wanting to talk, to offer help, more food, even perhaps homes. They finished the food and went off, without looking at her. She had sat down: it was in an old warehouse near the Underground entrance, where grass and shrubs were growing up through the floor, a place both sheltered and open, so that she could run for it if she had to. And she did have to . . . as she sat there, she saw that all around her were the children, creeping closer. They had bows and arrows. She, unable to believe, as she put it, "that they really were past hope," had talked quietly to them, of what she could offer, of what they risked living as they did. She understood, and with real terror, that *they did not understand her.* No, it was not that they did not understand speech, for they were communicating with each other in words that were recognisable, if only just—they *were* words, and not grunts and barks and screams. She sat on, knowing that an impulse would be enough to lift a bow up and send an arrow her way. She talked for as long as she could make herself. It was like, she said, talking into a vacuum; it was the most uncanny experience of her life. "When I looked at them, they were only kids—that was what I couldn't get into my thick head; they were just children . . . but they are wicked. In the end I got up and left. And the thing that was worst of all was when one of them came running after me and tugged at my skirt. I couldn't believe it. I knew he would have stuck a knife into me as easily. He had his finger in his mouth, pulling at my skirt. He was grinning. It was just an impulse, do you see? He didn't know what he was doing. The next minute there was a yell and they were all after me. I ran, I can tell you, and I only escaped by nipping into that old Park Hotel, at the corner, and I shook them off by barricading myself into a room on the fourth floor until dark."

These were the children Gerald had decided must be rescued by his household. Where would they all fit in? Well, somewhere, and if they didn't, there was that other big house just across the road, and perhaps Emily and he could run the two houses between them?

There was much resistance to the idea. From everybody. Emily, too. But Gerald wore them down: he always did, because after all it was he who maintained them, got food and supplies—he who took responsibility. If he said it could be done, then perhaps . . . and they were just "little kids"; he was right about that. "Just little kids, how can we let them rot out there?"

I believe that the others in the house comforted themselves with "They won't come anyway." They were wrong. Gerald could make people believe in him. He went down the Underground, heavily armed and showing it. Yes, he was terrified . . . they crept from holes and corners and tunnels; they seemed able to see without much light, whereas he was half-blinded by the flare of the torch. He was alone down there, and he was an enemy, since everybody was, offering them something they did not even know the words for. But he was able to make them follow him. He walked back from the Underground like a Pied Piper, and the twenty or so children who followed him ran and shouted all over the house, flinging open doors and slamming them, putting their fists through the precious polythene in the windows. Smelling food being cooked, they stood crowded together waiting for it to come their way. They saw people sitting down, children their own age with the adults, a sight that was astonishing to them. They

were subdued, it seemed; or at least their reflexes were temporarily put out. Or perhaps they were curious? They would
not sit down at table—they never had. They would not sit
down on the floor in an orderly way to be served, but they
did stand snatching at food which was passed to them on trays,
and bolted it down, their bright hard eyes watching everything,
trying to understand. When there was not enough food to fill
their aroused expectations, they ran shrieking and jeering
through the house, destroying everything.

At once that household broke up. Gerald would not listen
to reason, to the appeals of the existing inhabitants. There
was something about the situation of those children which
Gerald could not tolerate; he had to have them in there, he
had to try, and now he would not throw them out. By then
it was too late. The others left. It took a few hours for Gerald
and Emily to find their "family" all gone, while they were
house-parents of children who were savages. Gerald had apparently actually believed that they could be taught rules which
had been made for everyone's sake. Rules? They could hardly
understand what was said: they had no idea of a house as a
machine. They wrecked everything, tore up the vegetables
in the garden, sat at windows throwing filth at passers-by like
monkeys. They were drunk; they had taught themselves
drunkenness.

From my window, I saw that Emily had her arm in
bandages, and went over to ask what was wrong.

"Oh, nothing much," said she, with her dry little humour,
and then told how she and Gerald, descending that morning
to the lower regions of the house, had found the children
squatting and scratching all together, like monkeys in a too
small cage. There were bits of half-cooked meat about. They
had been roasting rats: near the house was an entrance to some

sewers. Nothing *under* the earth could be alien to these children, and they had crept down there with their catapults and bows and arrows.

Upstairs, Emily and Gerald had had a talk about tactics. Their situation was bleak. They had not been able to find any of their own children—not one. These had all left for other communes or households, or had decided that this was the moment to join a caravan going out of the city for good. The two were completely alone with these new children. They at last decided that a sharp business-like descent into the lower part of the house, and a reasonable but stern talk, must be attempted. What they envisaged was, in fact, the immemorial "sensible" talk of adults appealing to children's better sense before retribution had to fall. The trouble was, no retribution was possible; everything had already happened to these outcasts. Emily and Gerald realised they had nothing to threaten them with, and nothing to offer but the old arguments that life is more comfortable for a community if the members keep the place clean, share work, respect each other's individuality. And the children had survived without such thoughts ever having come near them.

But, not being able to think of anything else, the two young parents did go down, and one of the brats had suddenly run at Emily and hit her with a cudgel. Had hit her again and shouted—in a moment another little child had jumped in to attack. Gerald, going to rescue Emily, had found himself, too, being hit, bitten, scratched, and by a dozen or so of them. It had taken all their strength to fight off these children, not one of whom was over ten, and yet the inhibition against hitting or hurting a child was so strong that it "paralysed our arms," as Emily explained. "How can you hit a child?" Gerald had demanded, even though Emily's arm was badly bruised.

Standing there, embattled, blood all over the place, the two young people had fended off children, and, screaming above their screams, had tried to reason and persuade. The response to these exhortations was that the children had got themselves into a tight knot in a corner of the room, facing out, teeth bared, holding their cudgels ready to repel an attack, as if the words had been missiles. At last Emily and Gerald removed themselves, had another discussion, decided more must be attempted, but did not know what. That night, lying in their bed at the top of the house, they smelled smoke: the children had set fire to the ground floor, just as if the house were not their shelter. The fire was put out, and again the little savages cowered behind their weapons while Gerald, beside himself with emotion—for he simply could not endure that these children were not to be saved (for what, of course, was a question not one of us would ask)—Gerald pleaded and reasoned and persuaded. A stone from a catapult just missed his eye, and cut open his cheekbone.

What was to be done?

The children could not be thrown out. Who was to throw them out? No, with his own hands, Gerald had opened the gates to the invaders, who would now stay. Why not! They had piles of bedding, clothing, a fireplace to burn fuel in— they had never been warm before. Yes, almost certainly the house would soon burn down. It had been tidy and clean; now there was food everywhere, on floor, walls, ceilings. It stank of shit: the children used landings, even the rooms they slept in. They did not even have the cleanliness of animals, their instincts for responsibility. In every way they were worse than animals, and worse than men.

They menaced everyone in the neighbourhood, and there was to be a big meeting about it tomorrow on the pavement.

People were coming from the flats and from the houses round about. I was invited. That the barriers were completely down between the citizens and the life on the pavement showed how serious a threat these children were.

Next afternoon I went out, careful to leave Hugo in my bedroom, the door locked, the curtains drawn.

It was an autumn afternoon, the sun low and cold. Leaves were flying everywhere. We stood in a great mass, five hundred or more, and people kept coming in to join us. On a little improvised platform of bricks were the half-dozen leaders. Emily was up there with Gerald.

Before the talking began, the children who were to be discussed arrived and stood a little apart, listening. There were now about forty of them. I remember that we were all encouraged they were with us, had come at all—community feeling of a kind, perhaps? At least they had understood there was to be a meeting that concerned them; they had taken in words, and understood them in the same way we did. . . . Then they began stamping around and chanting, "I am the king of the castle, you are a dirty rascal." It was terrifying. This ancient children's song was a war-song; they had made it one, they were living it. But, more than that, we could all see how familiar words could slip out of key—how quickly things could change, we could change. . . . *Had* changed: those children were ourselves. We knew it. We stood there, sullen and uncomfortable, listening. It was in accompaniment to this shrill jeering chant that Gerald began to describe the situation. Meanwhile there was apprehension, a restlessness in the crowd, which was due to more than the presence of the children, or our knowledge of ourselves. For this was like a "mass meeting" of the ordinary world, and we had every reason to fear such meetings. Above all, what we feared more than any-

thing was the attention of Authority—that "they" should be
alerted. Gerald, reasonable as he always was, explained how
essential it was for the sake of every one of us to rescue the
children, and we, standing shoulder to shoulder, again listening
to a person talking down at us from a platform, were thinking
that this was one street in one of many suburbs, that our comfortable habit of seeing only ourselves, our pavements, and their
energetic life was a way of being able to cope with the fear. A
useful way: we were not important, and the city was large. We
were able to continue our precarious little lives because of our
good sense, which enabled "them" to take no notice of us.
What they chose to overlook was more all the time; but they
still would not stand for the burning down of a house or a
street, or for a gang of children who were under no one's control, terrorising everyone. They had their spies among us.
They knew what went on.

Perhaps—in describing, as I have done, only what went
on among ourselves, in our neighbourhood—I have not been
able to give a clear enough picture of how our by now very
remarkable society worked . . . for, after all, it *was* working.
All this time, while ordinary life simply dissolved away,
or found new shapes, the structure of government continued,
though heavy and cumbersome and becoming all the time
more ramified. Nearly everyone who had a job at all was in
administration—yes, of course we ordinary people joked that
the machinery of government was maintained so that privileged
folk could have jobs and salaries. And there was some truth
in it. What government really did was to adjust itself to events,
while pretending, probably even to itself, that it initiated
them. And the law courts worked on, plenty of them; the
processes of law were infinitely tricky and prolonged, or sudden and Draconian, as if the impatience of the practitioners

of law with their own processes and precedents got itself impressed by the way law could suddenly be dispensed with altogether, be overridden and rewritten—and then what had been substituted went grinding along as heavily as before. The prisons were as full as ever, though expedients were always being found to empty them: so many crimes were being committed, and there seemed to be new unforeseen categories of crime every day. Reform schools, Borstals, welfare homes, old-age homes—all these proliferated, and they were savage and dreadful places.

Everything worked. Worked somehow. Worked on an edge, on one side of which was what authority tolerated, on the other what it could not: this meeting was well over the edge. And very soon the police would arrive in a fleet of cars and drag off these children and put them behind bars in a "home" where they wouldn't survive a week. Nobody, knowing their history, could feel anything but compassion for them; not one of us wished for them an end in a "home"—but neither did we want, we could not tolerate, a visit of the police which would bring to official notice a hundred living arrangements that were not legal. Houses being lived in by people who didn't own them, gardens growing food for people who had no right to eat it, the ground floors of deserted houses accommodating horses and donkeys which were transport for the innumerable little businesses that illegally flourished, the little businesses themselves, where all the riches of our old technology were being so ingeniously adapted and transformed, minuscule turkey farms, chicken runs, rabbit sheds—all this new life, like growth pushing up under trees, was illegal. None of it should exist. None of it, officially, existed; and when "they" were forced into seeing these things, they sent in troops or the police to sweep it all away. Such a visit would be referred to in a headline, a broadcast, a newscast as "Such-and-Such Street was cleaned out today." And everyone knew what had happened and thanked fortune it was someone else's street.

Such a "clean-out" was what everybody feared more than anything, and yet we were tempting "them" by gathering together. Gerald talked on, in an emotional desperate way, as if the act of talking itself could produce some solution. He said at one point that the only way to cope with the "kids" was to separate them and put them into households in ones and twos. I remember the jeering that went up from the children, and their white angry faces. They stopped their pathetic war-dance and stood huddled, facing outwards, weapons at the ready.

A young man appeared over the heads of the crowd; he had his arm around the trunk of a tree and was holding himself there. "What are we doing this for?" he shouted. "If they came now, that would be the end of us—never mind about those kids. And if you want to know what I think, we should inform the police and be done with it. We can't cope with it. Gerald has tried—haven't you, Gerald?"

And he disappeared, sliding down the trunk.

Emily now spoke. It looked as if someone had asked her to. She stood on the pile of bricks, serious, worried, and said, "What can you expect? These kids defend themselves. That's what they have learned. Perhaps we should persevere with them? I'll volunteer if others will."

"No, no, no" came from everywhere in the crowd. Someone shouted out, "You've got a broken arm from them, by the look of it."

"Rumour broke the arm, not the kids," said Emily, smiling, and a few people laughed.

And there we stood. It is not often a crowd so large can remain silent, in indecision. To call the police would be a real

descent away from what we could tolerate in ourselves, and we
could not bring ourselves to do it.

A man shouted, "I'll call the police myself, and you can
have it out with me afterwards. We've got to do it, or the
whole neighbourhood will go up in flames one of these nights."

And now the children themselves began edging away,
still in their tight little band, clutching their sticks, their
stones, their catapults.

Someone shouted, "They're off!" They were. The crowd
jostled and swayed, trying to see how the children ran across
the road and disappeared into the dusk.

"Shame," called a woman from the crowd. "They're
scared, poor little mites."

At that moment there was a shout: "The Police!"—and
everyone was running. From the windows of my flat, Gerald
and Emily and I and some others watched the great cars come
roaring up, their lights flashing, their sirens shrieking. There
was no one on the pavement. The cars drove by in a pack,
around a block, and then back and around again. The shrieking, whining, clanging posse of monsters drove around and
about our silent streets for half an hour or so, "showing their
teeth," as we said, and then they went away.

What "they" could not tolerate, could not tolerate even
now, was even the semblance of a public meeting, which might
threaten them. Extraordinary and pathetic, for the last thing
that interested anyone by this time was changing the form of
government: we wanted only to forget it.

When the streets were quiet, Emily and Gerald went
off to the other house to see if the children had gone back there.
But they had been and gone, taking with them all their little
belongings—sticks and stones and weapons, bits of roast rat,
uncooked potatoes.

The two had the house to themselves. There was nothing

to prevent a new community being made there. The old one
might be restored? No, of course it could not: something or-
ganic, which had grown naturally, had been destroyed.


□   □   □


It was cold. There was very little fuel. In the long darkening afternoons and evenings, I sat with a single candle glimmering in my room. Or I would put it out and let the fire
light the room.

Sitting there one day, staring at the fire-flicker, I was
through it and beyond—into the most incongruous scene you
could imagine. How can I say "ill-timed" of a world where
time did not exist? All the same, even there, where one took
what came, did not criticise the order of things, I was thinking,
What a strange scene to show itself now!

I was with Hugo. Hugo was not just my accompaniment,
an aide, as a dog is. He was a being, a person, in his own right,
and necessary to the events I was seeing.

It was a girl's room, a schoolgirl's. Rather small, with conventional flowered curtains, a white spread for the bed, a desk
with schoolbooks laid tidily, a school timetable pinned on a
white cupboard. In the room, in front of a mirror that ordinarily was not part of the room at all—it had a little looking-
glass tacked to the wall above a wash-basin; a long, capacious
mirror all scrolled and gilded and curlicued and fluted, the
sort of mirror one associated with a film set or a smart dress
shop or the theatre—in front of this mirror, here only because
the atmosphere and emotional necessities of the scene needed
more than the sober small square looking-glass, was a young

woman. Was Emily, a girl presented or parcelled up as a
young woman.

Hugo and I stood side by side, looking at her. My hand
was on the beast's neck, and I could feel the tremors of his
disquiet coming up into my hand from his misgiving heart.
Emily was fourteen or so, but "well-grown," as once they had
been used to put it. She was in evening dress. The dress was
scarlet. It is hard to describe what my feelings were on seeing
it, seeing her. They were certainly violent. I was shocked by the
dress—or, rather, that such dresses had ever been tolerated,
ever been worn by any woman, because of what they made of
the woman. But they had been taken for granted, had been
seen as just another fashion, no worse or better than any.

The dress was tight around waist and bust: the word "bust"
is accurate; those weren't breasts that breathed and lifted or
drooped and could change with emotion, or the month's
changes: they made a single, inflated, bulging mound. Shoulders and back were naked. The dress was tight to the knees
over hips and bottom—again the accurate word, for Emily's
buttocks were rounded out into a single protuberance. Below,
it twirled and flared around her ankles. It was a dress of blatant
vulgarity. It was also, in a perverted way, non-sexual, for all
its advertisement of the body, and embodied the fantasies of
a certain kind of man who, dressing a woman thus, made her
a doll, ridiculous, both provocative and helpless; disarmed
her, made her something to hate, to pity, to fear—a grotesque.
In this monstrosity of a dress, which was a conventional garment worn by hundreds of thousands of women within my
lifetime, coveted by women, admired by women in innumerable mirrors, used by women to clothe their masochistic fantasies—inside this scarlet horror stood Emily, turning her head
this way and that before the glass. Her hair was "up," leaving
her nape bare. She had scarlet nails. In Emily's lifetime the

fashion had never been thus; there had been no fashion at all, at least for ordinary people, but here she was, a few paces from us, and, sensing us there, her faithful animal and her anxious guardian, she turned her head, slow, slow, and looked at us with long lowered lashes, her lips held apart for fantasy kisses. Into the room came the large tall woman, Emily's mother, and her appearance at once diminished Emily, made her smaller, so that she began to dwindle from the moment the mother stood there. Emily faced her and, as she shrank in size, acted out her provocative sex, writhing and letting her tongue protrude from her mouth. The mother gazed, horrified, full of dislike, while her daughter got smaller and smaller, was a tiny scarlet doll, with its pouting bosom, its bottom outlined from waist to knees. The little doll twisted and postured, and then vanished in a flash of red smoke, like a morality tale of the flesh and the devil.

Hugo moved forward into the space before the mirror and sniffed and smelled at it, and then at the floor where Emily had stood. The mother's face was twisted with dislike, but now it was this beast that was affecting her so. "Go away," she said, in a low breathless voice—that voice squeezed out of us by an extremity of dislike or fear. "Go away, you dirty filthy animal." And Hugo retreated to me; we backed away together before the advancing woman, who had her fist raised to hit me, to hit Hugo. We backed away, fast, then faster, while the woman advanced, grew large, became enormous, absorbing into herself Emily's girlhood room, with its simpering conventionality, the incongruous mirror, and—snap!—we were back in the living-room, in the dark place where the single candle bloomed in its hollow of light, where the small fire warmed a little space of air around it. I was sitting in my usual place. Hugo was near the wall, looking at me. We looked at each other. He was whimpering—no, the right word is crying.

He was crying, in desolation, as a human does. He turned and crept away into my bedroom.

And that was the last time I saw Emily there in what I have called the "personal." I mean that I did not again enter scenes that showed her development as a girl, or baby, or child. That horrible mirror-scene, with its implications of perversity, was the end. Nor, entering that other world through— and this was new, too—the flames, or the husbanded glow of the fire as I sat beside it through these long autumn nights, did I find the rooms which opened and opened out from each other: or I did not think I had. Returning from a trip into that place, I could not keep a clear memory of what I had experienced, where I had been. I would know that I *had* been there, from the emotions that sustained, or were draining, me: I had been fed there from some capacious murmuring source all comfort and sweetness; I had been frightened and threatened. Or perhaps in, or under, the thick light of this room seemed now to shimmer another light which came from *there;* I had brought it with me and it stayed for a while, making me long for what it represented.

And when it faded, how slow and dim and heavy was the air. . . . Hugo had developed a dry cough, and as we sat together, he might suddenly jump up and go to the window, nosing at it, his sides labouring, and I would open it, realising that I, too, was in a stupor from the fug and the heaviness of the room. We would stand side by side, breathing the air that flowed in from outside, trying to flush our lungs clean with it.

□   □   □

After some days when I had not seen Emily at all, I went to Gerald's house through streets which were disordered, as

always, but seemed much cleaner. It was as if an excess of
dirtiness and mess had erupted everywhere, but then winds, or
at least movements of air, had taken some of it away. I saw
no one during this walk.

I half expected to find that efforts had been made towards
restoring the vegetable garden. No. It was wrecked and
trampled, and some chickens were at work in it. A dog was
creeping towards them under the bushes. This was so rare a
sight that I had to stop and look. Not one dog, but a pack of
dogs, and they were creeping on all sides towards the pecking
chickens. I cannot tell you how uneasy this made me; there
was something enormous waiting to burst in on me, some real
movement and change in our situation. Dogs!—a pack of dogs,
eleven or twelve of them—what could it possibly mean? And,
watching them, my prickling skin and the cold sweat on my
forehead told me I was afraid, and had good reason to be: the
dogs could choose me instead of the chickens. I went as fast
as I could inside the house. Which was clean and empty.
Ascending through the house, I was listening for life in
the rooms off the landings—nothing. At the top of the
house a closed door. I knocked and Emily opened it a crack
—saw it was me, and let me in, shutting it fast again and
bolting it. She was dressed in furs, trousers of rabbit or cat,
a fur jacket, a grey fur cap pulled low over her face. She
looked like a pantomime cat. But pale, and sorrowful. Where
was Gerald?

She returned to a nest she had made for herself on the
floor, of fur rugs and fur cushions. The room smelled like a den
from the furs, but sniffing, trying it out, I realised that otherwise the air was fresh and sharp, and that I was breathing in
great gasps. Emily made a place for me in the rugs, and I
sat and covered myself. It was very cold: no heating here. We
sat quietly together—breathing.

She said, "Now that the air outside has become impossible to breathe, I spend as much time as I can here."

And I understood it was true: this was a moment when someone said something which crystallised into fact intimations only partly grasped that had been pointing towards an obvious conclusion . . . in this case, it was that the air we breathed had indeed become hard on our lungs, had been getting fouler and thicker for a long time. We had become used to it, were adapting: I, like everyone else, had been taking short reluctant breaths, as if rationing what we took into our lungs, our systems, could also ration the poisons—what poisons? But who could know, or say! This was "it" again, in a new form—"it," perhaps, in its original form?

Sitting in that room, whose floor was all covered with furs for lying and reclining, a room in which there was nothing to do but to lie, or to sit, I realised that I was . . . happy simply to be there, and breathe. Which I did for a long time while my head cleared and my spirits lightened. I looked out through clean polythene at a thick sky turbulent with clouds that held snow; I watched the light changing on the wall. From time to time, Emily and I smiled at each other. It was very quiet everywhere. There came at one point a violent cackling and snarling from the garden, but we did not move. It ceased. Silence again.

There were machines in the room: one hanging from the ceiling, another on the floor, one nailed to a wall. These were for purifying the air, and they worked by sending out streams of electrons, negative ions; people had used them for some time, just as no one would dream of using water from the taps unless it had passed through one of the many types of water purifier. Air and water, water and air, the basics of our substance, the elements we swim in, move in, of which we are formed and re-formed, continuously, perpetually, re-created and renewed . . . for how long had we had to distrust them, evade them, treat them as possible enemies?

"You should take some machines home with you," she said. "There's a room full of them."

"Gerald?"

"Yes, he went to a warehouse. There's a room of them under this one. But I'll help you carry them. How can you live in that filthy air?" And she said this in the way one does to bring something out one has wanted to say but has kept back.

She was smiling—and reproachful.

"Are you coming back—" I hesitated to say "home," but she said, "Yes, I'll come home with you."

"Hugo will be pleased," I said, not meaning any reproach, but her eyes filled and she reddened.

"Why are you able to come now?" I asked, risking it; but she simply shook her head, meaning, I'll answer in a moment. . . . And she did, when she had taken herself into control.

"There's no point in my staying here now."

"Gerald has gone?"

"I don't know where he is. Not since he brought the machines."

"He is making a new gang for himself?"

"Trying to."

When she was on her feet, rolling up furs into big bundles to take with us, laying out others in which to wrap machines, there was a knock, and Emily went to see who it was. No, not Gerald, but a couple of children. At the sight of children, I was afraid. And I realised "in a flash"—another one!—that I, that everybody had come to see all children as, simply, terrifying. Even before the arrival of the "poor little kids" this had been true.

These two—dirty, bright-faced, sharp, wary—sat on the

fur-floor, apart from us, and apart from each other. Each held a heavy stick, with a nail-studded knob, ready for use against us, and against each other.

"Thought I'd get a breath of fresh air," said one, a red-headed boy, all milky skin and charming freckles. The other, a fair, angelic little girl, said, for herself, "Yes, I wanted some fresh air."

They sat and breathed and watched while we, keeping an eye on them, went on with the rolling and packing.

"Where are you going?" asked the girl.

"Tell Gerald he knows where to find me."

This gave me too much food for thought to absorb at once.

These children were part of Gerald's new gang? Were they not members of the gang of children from the Underground? If this was true, then . . . perhaps that gang was only lethal as a unit, but the individuals were savable, and Gerald had been right? When our packs were ready, we left, the children coming with us, but they left us on seeing the butcher's yard that was the garden: feathers everywhere, bits of flesh, a dead dog. The children were cutting up the dog as we left, squatting on either side of the carcass, at work with sharp bits of steel.

We returned through streets which I pointed out to Emily as being—surely?—less filthy, and noted her small checked reaction. Streets which had no one in them, not a soul apart from ourselves—I commented on this, too, and heard her sigh. She was being patient with me.

In the lobby of the building we lived in, a great vase that had held flowers was lying in fragments outside the lift. There was a dead rat among the rubbish. As Emily took the animal by the tail to throw it out into the street, Professor White, Mrs. White, and Janet came along the corridor we jointly used. They had so far retained old ways that it was possible to say at once they were dressed for travelling—coats, scarves, suitcases. Seeing them thus, all three together, was a reminder of that other world or stratum of society, above ours, where people still presented themselves through clothes or belongings, for occasions. The Whites, as if nothing had happened to our world, were off on a journey, and Janet was saying, "Oh, quick, do let's go—let's go, Mummy, Daddy. It's so horrid being here when there's no one left." *Click*—there it was again, the few words flung out, emitted as if by the atmosphere itself, by "it," summing up a new state of affairs that had not yet got itself summed up—or at least not by me. I saw Emily's shrewd little glance at me, and she even instinctively moved a step closer, in a maternal gesture of protection for what might be a moment of weakness. I stood silent, watching the Whites fuss and arrange, seeing my past, our pasts: it looked comic. It *was* comic. We always had been ridiculous, little self-important animals, acting our roles, playing our parts. . . . It was not pretty, watching the Whites, and seeing oneself. And then we all said goodbye, quite in the old style: it was nice to know you, I hope we'll meet again—all that kind of thing, as if nothing much was happening. They had discovered that a coach was going out of the city that afternoon, ten miles to the north, on some kind of official business. Not for the use of ordinary citizens, but they had bribed and urged their way into being on this coach, which would set them down a mile from the airport, with their luggage. An official flight was scheduled for the extreme north this afternoon: again, while no ordinary person could ever get on such a flight, the head of a department and his family might just manage it, if they had the money—astronomical, of course—not for fares but, again, for bribes. What bartering and promises and threats

and appeals must have gone into this journey, what a fearful
effort—and all of it entirely in the new style, our new mode,
that of survival, of surviving at all costs—but not a trace of this
showed in their manner: Goodbye, goodbye, it was nice to have
you both as neighbours; see you soon, perhaps; yes, I do hope
so; goodbye, pleasant journey.

We went into my flat, and from the windows watched
them walk down the street carrying their heavy cases.

The rooms next to mine would be empty now. Empty . . .
it occurred to me that I had been seeing very few people
around in the lobby, the corridors. What had happened to the
market? I asked Emily and she shrugged, clearly feeling that
I ought to know. I left my flat again, and went to the janitor's
room down the passage. "In case of emergency, apply to Flat
7, 5th Floor." The way the notice hung there crooked, the
silence from behind the door, told me that he and his family
had gone off, had left; that notice might have been there for
weeks. But I went to the lift, which did sometimes work, and
pressed the bell. The machine shifted somewhere above, and
I waited on, pressing and peering, but the lift did not come,
so I used the stairs, up and up, floor after floor empty, with no
liveliness of trading and bartering anywhere. The traders, the
buyers, the goods—all were gone, and there was nobody in
Flat 7, on the fifth floor; but at the top of the building, near
the roof, I saw youngsters feeding horses with pitchforks of
hay, and I retreated, not wanting to be seen, since some of
those at work were young children. I crept down that passage,
passing more rooms that held animals: a goat's head peered
around a door, a pair of kingly lambs stood at the end of the
corridor, and there was a shovelling and scraping from somewhere close and the smell of pigs. I tried the roof itself: up
here was a flourishing market garden, with vegetables and

herbs of all kinds, a polythene greenhouse, rabbits in cages, and a family—mother, father, and three children—hard at work. They gave me the look of that time: *Who are you? Friend? Enemy?*—and waited, their implements held ready to use as weapons. Down I went again to the floor beneath, and a child froze into a dark corner—he had been following me. His teeth were bared in a vindictive but calculated grin. I mean that the animosity was calculated, measured, so as to scare me. I could imagine him with a looking-glass he had picked up in some corner, practising a variety of horrible expressions. I was indeed frightened: his hand (like Emily's these days!) was held close to his chest, where the handle of a knife showed. I thought I knew his face, believed—he was red-haired and the right size —he was one of the urchins who had visited Emily that same day. But of course I made no appeal on such sentimental grounds as acquaintance, but glared back, and moved my right hand threateningly to where my—non-existent—knife was. He held his ground, and I walked on past him down the passage, looking into rooms, feeling him creep behind me, but at a good distance. I saw Gerald. He was sitting on heaps of furs surrounded by children: they were the "Underground gang" and they were living in "my" building. This gave me a real shock, and I went downstairs, boldly passing the little boy, who was keeping up his business of scowling and threatening. Down, down, and into my flat, which, after all I had seen, seemed a strange little place of order, of old-fashioned amenities, of warmth. Emily had made up a fire, and was sitting next to it, opposite Hugo. They were looking at each other, not touching, looking long and quiet at each other. The girl entirely wrapped in furs, so it was hard to tell where her own glossy hair began and ended, and the poor beast, with his rough and yellow hide—Beauty and her Beast, in this guise,

but Beauty was so close to her Beast now, wrapped in beast's
clothing, as sharp and wary as a beast, surviving as one. Yes,
Beauty had been brought down, brought very low. . . . I had a
bad moment, watching the two there, thinking how very near
we were to running and scurrying like rats along tunnels—
but saw that the fire was solid and glowing, the air-machines
we had brought were all at work, and the curtains had been
drawn, with old blankets pinned over them. The air here was
good, and clean, and I could feel my real self coming alive
in it, but first I again left the flat and went out on the pavement. Dusk was coming down. Only a few people were on the
gathering-place. They loitered there with a lost uncertain
look: so many tribes had left, and these were the laggards. How
dark everything was! Usually, as dusk came down, hundreds
of candle flames seemed to float up and down and along the
great buildings: people at their windows, looking down, and
the rooms behind them shadowy in candlelight. But now, this
evening, there were a few little glimmers high up in the dark-
ness. From my windows nothing at all, yet my rooms were
still alive: it was not possible now to tell from lights at windows
who was in the building. No lights in the streets: only a thick
heavy dark, the glow of a cigarette on the pavement—otherwise nothing. I found that I was standing there visualising the
dark face of the building and a single candle flame—mine—
alive in it. So things had been recently. Anyone passing would
have known that here, alone, undefended, was a single person,
or a single family. I had been crazy. Emily's little checked reactions of impatience or concern were understandable, understood. And, often enough, in the glow of that single flame
must have been visible the patient watching outline of Hugo:
yes, it was just as well she had come home—this time, or so it
seemed, to look after me, not the other way around.

I went back into the flat. Emily had gone to bed. Hugo had not gone with her. Pride: and of course she would have understood it. He lay in front of the fire like any domestic beast, nose to the warmth, his green eyes watchful and open. I put my hand out to him and he allowed me a little tremor of his tail. I sat on for a long time, as the fire burned down, and listened to the absolute silence of the building. Yet above me was a farmyard, were animals, were the lethal children, was an old friend, Gerald: I went to bed, wrapping my head as peasants and simple people may do, against thoughts of danger, leaving just my face free—and woke next morning to find no water in the taps.

The building, as a machine, was dead.

That morning Gerald came down with two of the children, Redhair and a little black girl. He brought offerings of wine—for he had found an old wine merchant half-looted; and some blankets. Also, some food. Emily made the five of us some food, a porridge of some kind, with meat in it: it was good, and comforting.

Gerald wanted us to move to the top floor, where it would be easy for him to fix up a wind-machine, one of the little windmills: we would have enough power to heat water, when we could get it. I said nothing, let Emily do the talking, make choices. She said no, it would be better to stay down here: she did not look at me as she said this, and it slowly came into me the reason was that up at the top of the building we would be more vulnerable to attack: we could not run away easily up there, whereas here it would be a question of jumping out of a window. This was why she said no to his offer of "a large flat—really, Emily, very big—and full of all sorts of food and stuff. And I could fix it up with power in a day—couldn't we?" He appealed to the children, who nodded and grinned.

They sat on either side of him, those little things, about seven or eight years old: they were his, his creatures; he had made himself theirs; he had his gang, his tribe . . . but at the cost of doing what they wanted, serving them.

What he really wanted was to have her back. He wanted her to go up with him, to live with him—as queen, or chief lady, or brigand's woman—among the children, his gang. And she did not want this; she most definitely did not. Not that she said it, but it was clear. And the children, sharp-eyed and alert, knew what the issue was. It was hard to know what they felt —there were none of the familiar signals to tell us. Their eyes turned from Emily to Gerald, from Gerald to Emily: they were wondering if Emily, like Gerald, could become one of them, kill with them, fight with them? Or they were thinking that she was pretty and nice and it would be pleasant to have her around with them? They saw her, or felt her, as filling the place of their mothers—if they remembered mothers, a family, at all? They were thinking that they should kill her, because of Gerald's—their possession's—love of her? Who could say?

Their eating habits were disgusting. Gerald said, "Use a spoon—look, like this. . . . No, don't throw it on the floor," in a way that showed that in his own rooms, his own cave, he no longer bothered with such niceties. His glance at Emily said that if she would be there with them, she could influence and civilise. . . . But it was all no use, and the three, the man and the two little children, went off at midday. They would bring us fresh meat tomorrow: a sheep was going to be killed. He would come and see Emily soon: he spoke to her; it was Emily's place now. My flat was Emily's, and I was her elderly attendant. Well, why not?

She was silent when he had gone, and then Hugo came

and sat with his face on her knee: he was saying, *I can see that you have really chosen me at last, me against him, me instead of all the others!*

It was funny and pathetic; but she flashed me glances that I was not to laugh: it was she who suppressed smiles, bit her lips, breathed deep to hold down laughter. She fussed and caressed: "Dear Hugo, dear, dear Hugo. . . ." I noted, and watched. I was seeing a mature woman, a woman who has had her fill of everything, but is still being asked from, demanded of, persuaded into giving: such a woman is generous indeed; her coffers and wells are always full and being given out. She loves—oh, yes, but somewhere in her is a deadly weariness. She has known it all, and doesn't want any more—but what can she do? She knows herself—the eyes of men and boys say so—as a source; if she is not this, then she is nothing. So she still thinks—she has not yet shed that delusion. She gives. She gives. But with this weariness held in check and concealed. . . . So she stroked her Hugo's head, made love to his ears, whispered affectionate nonsense to him. Over his head, her eyes met mine: they were the eyes of a mature woman of about thirty-five, or forty; she would never willingly suffer any of it again. Like the jaded woman of our dead civilisation, she knew love like a fever, to be suffered, to be lived through: "falling in love" was an illness to be endured, a trap which might lead her to betray her own nature, her good sense, and her real purposes. It was not a door to anything but itself: not a key to living. It was a state, a condition, sufficient unto itself, almost independent of its object . . . "being in love." If she *had* spoken of it, she would have spoken of it so, as I've written. But she did not want to talk. She exuded her weariness, her willingness to give out if absolutely necessary, to give without belief. Gerald, whom she had adored, the "first love" of tradi-

tion; for whom she had waited, suffered, lain awake at nights
—Gerald, her lover, now needed and wanted her, having
worked through the cycle of *his* needs, but she no longer had
the energy to rise and meet him.

When, later that day, Gerald came down again, alone, in
an attempt to persuade her to return with him, she did talk
to him. She talked and he listened. She told him what had
happened to him, for he did not know.

After the community he had built up in his house had
been broken up by the gang of "kids" from the Underground,
and when he had seen that none of his own household would
return, he had put all his effort into getting Emily to stay with
him, to make a new household. He had returned to the pavement, to attract the nucleus of a new tribe. But this did not
happen, it had not happened. Why? Perhaps it was believed
that he was in contact with the dangerous children, or that
any new community he formed must attract them; perhaps the
fact he had shown openly that he was prepared to settle for one
woman, for Emily—instead of being free in his choices, bestow-
ing favours on whomever he found in his bed—put off the girls.
Whatever law it was that operated, the result was that Gerald,
formerly a young prince, perhaps the most regarded of all the
young men on the pavement, found himself unfollowed, merely
one of the youngsters who had to attach himself to a leader
in order to survive. . . . Gerald listened to all this, thoughtful,
attentive, disagreeing with nothing Emily was saying.

"And then you decided it was better to have the children
than to have nothing, or to be patient and wait. You simply
had to have a gang at all costs. And you went back to them
and took them over. But they have taken *you* over—can't you
see? I bet you have to do exactly what they want, don't you?
I am sure you never can stop them doing anything they want?
And you have to go along with whatever it is?"

But now he had retreated, was not prepared to take this, could not listen.

"But they are just little kids," he said. "Isn't it better for them that they have me? I get them food and things. I look after them."

"They had food and things before," Emily said dryly.

Too dry . . . he saw her as critical of him—that, and nothing more. There was no affection for him—so he felt it. Off he went, and did not come again for some days.

We were organising our life, our rooms.

We were supplied with clean air at the cost of sitting and turning a handle to recharge batteries from time to time. It was warm: Emily went out with an axe and returned with great bundles of wood. And, just as I was thinking that the shortage of water would drive us to the roads, there was a clop-clopping outside, and a donkey cart made its appearance loaded with plastic buckets of water, wooden buckets, metal buckets.

"Wa-a-a-ter! Wa-a-a-ter!" The old cry sounded through our damp northern streets. Two girls of about eleven were selling the stuff—or, rather, bartering. I went out with containers, and saw other people coming from the various blocks of flats around us. Not many, not more than fifty or so in all. I bought water dearly: the little girls had learned to be hard, to shake their heads and shrug at the prospect that people would do without water. For two buckets of good water—we were at least allowed to taste it before buying—I paid a sheepskin.

And then Gerald appeared, with about twenty of his gang —they came with containers of every sort. Of course, there were all those animals up there needing water: but in a moment the gang had taken the water, simply grabbed it: they did not pay. I found myself shouting at Gerald that it was their livelihood, the little girls'—but he took no notice. I think he did not hear me. He stood on the alert, all vigilance, his eyes coldly assessing, while his children lifted down the buckets and ran off into the building with them, while the sellers complained, and the people who had come to buy water and had not yet been served stood shouting and screaming. Then Gerald and the children had gone and it was my turn to be robbed. I stood with two filled buckets, and one of the men from the block of flats opposite held out his hand, lowering his head to glare into my eyes, baring his teeth. I handed over one bucket and ran indoors with the other. Emily had been watching through the window. She seemed sad. Also irritated: I could see the words she would use to scold Gerald forming in her mind.

A dish of clean water was put down for Hugo and he drank and drank. He stood beside the empty dish, head lowered: we filled it again, and he drank. . . . A third of the bucket went in this way, and in our minds was the same thought—Hugo's, as well as ours. Emily sat by him and put her arms around him in the old way: he was not to worry or grieve, she would protect him, no one would attack him; he would have water if she had to go without or if I did. . . .

When the water sellers came a couple of days later, they had men guarding the water with guns, and we bought in orderly queues. Gerald and his gang were not there. A woman in the queue said that "that rotten lot" had opened up the Fleet River, and had started selling water on their own account. It was true, and for us—Hugo, Emily, and me—a good turn of events, for Gerald brought us down a bucket of water every day and sometimes more.

"Well, we had to do it—we have to keep our animals watered, don't we?"

From the defensiveness of this, we knew that some hard battle had been fought. With the authorities? With other people using that source? For of course old wells and springs had been opened everywhere over the city. If with the authorities, then how was it that Gerald and the children had won —they must have done, to be able to reach and tap the supply.

"Well," said Gerald, "they haven't got enough troops to keep an eye on everything, have they? Most of them have gone, haven't they? I mean, there are more of us than there are of them now. . . ."

□  □  □

And if everyone had gone, what were we—Emily and Hugo and I—doing here?

But we no longer thought about leaving, not seriously. We might talk a little about the Dolgellys, or say: "Well, one of these days we really ought to be thinking . . ."

Air, water, food, warmth—we had them all. Things were easier now than they had been for a long time. There was less stress, less danger. And even the few people who were still lodged in the cracks and crevices of this great city kept leaving, leaving. . . .

I watched a tribe go off as the autumn ended and winter came down. The last tribe, at least from our pavements. It was like all the others I had seen go, but better equipped, and typical of the caravans from our particular area: now, comparing notes, it seems that each neighbourhood had its peculiarities of travel, even styles! Yes, I can use that word . . . how quickly customs and habits do grow up! I remember hearing someone say, and this was quite in the early days of the departing tribes, "Where is the shoe leather? We *always* have a supply of shoe leather."

Perhaps it would be of interest if I described this late departure in more detail.

It was cold that morning. A low sky moved fast from west to east, a dark, pouring sea. The air was thick, and hard to breathe, although there was a wind stirring and rolling drifts of the snow crumbs that lightly surfaced road and pavements. The ground seemed fluid. The tall buildings all around showed sharp and dark, or disappeared in snow flurries and cloud.

About fifty people had gathered, all rolled tightly into their furs. At the front were two young men with the two guns they owned prominently in evidence. Behind them came four more, with bows and arrows, sticks, knives. Then came a cart converted from a motorcar: everything taken off down to wheel-level, and boards laid over these to make a surface. The cart was being drawn by a horse, and on it were piled bundles of clothes and equipment, three small children, and hay for the horse. The older children were expected to walk.

Behind this cart walked the women and children, and behind them came another cart, and in the yokes were two youths. On this cart was a large version of the old haybox: a wooden container, insulated and padded, into which could be fitted pots which, taken off the boil just before the start of a journey, would go on simmering inside their nests and be ready to provide a meal at its end. After this second cart came a third, an old milk cart carrying food supplies: grains, dried vegetables, concentrates, and so on. And a fourth cart, drawn by a donkey. It was arranged for cages. There were some laying hens. There were rabbits, not for eating but for breeding: a dozen or so impregnated does. This last cart had a special guard of four armed boys.

It was the horse and the donkey that distinguished this caravan: our part of the city was known for its draft animals. Why we developed this speciality I don't know. Perhaps it was because there were riding stables in the old days, and these developed into breeding establishments when there was a need. Even our little common had horses on it—under heavy guard night and day, of course.

Usually, when a column of people left for the journey north or west, people came out of the buildings to say goodbye, to wish them well, to send messages to friends and relatives who had gone on ahead. That morning only four people came. Hugo and I sat quietly in our window watching as the tribe arranged itself and left, without fuss or farewells. Very different this departure from earlier ones, which had been so boisterous and gay. These people were subdued, seemed apprehensive, made themselves small and inconspicuous inside their furs: this caravan of theirs would make rich booty.

Emily did not even watch.

At the very last moment, Gerald came out with half a dozen of the children, and they stood on the pavement until the last cart with its cackling load had gone out of sight beyond the church at the corner. Gerald turned then, and led his flock back inside the building. He saw me and nodded, but without smiling. He looked strained—as well he might. Even to see that band of infant savages was enough to make one's stomach muscles tighten in anxiety. And he lived among them, day and night: I believe he had run out with them to stop them attacking the loaded carts.

That night there was a knock on the door, and four of the children stood there: they were wild-eyed and excited. Emily

simply shut the door on them and locked it. Then she put
heavy chairs against it. A scuffling and whispering—the footsteps retreated.

Emily looked at me, and mouthed over Hugo's head—it
took me a few moments to work it out—"Roast Hugo."

"Or roast Emily," I said.

A few minutes later, we heard screams coming from
along the street, then the sound of many rushing feet, and
children's shrill voices in triumph—all the sounds of a raid, a
crime. We pushed aside our heavy curtains and were in
time to see, through a glimmer from the snow that was being
lit by a small moon, Gerald's gang, but without Gerald, dragging something up the front steps. It looked like a body. It
need not have been anything of the kind, could have been a
sack or a bundle. But the suspicion was there, and strong
enough to make us believe it.

We sat on through the night quietly by our fire, waiting,
listening.

There was nothing to prevent one or all of us becoming
victims at any moment.

Nothing. Not the fact that Gerald, by himself or with
a selection of the children, or even some of the children by
themselves, might come down to visit us in the most normal
way in the world. They brought us gifts. They brought flour
and dried milk and eggs; sheets of polythene, cellotape, nails,
tools of all kinds. They gave us fur rugs, coal, seeds, candles.
They brought . . . the city around was almost empty, and all
one had to do was to walk into unguarded buildings and warehouses and take what one fancied. But most of what was there
were things no one would ever use again or want to: things
about which, in a few years' time, if some survivor found them,
he would have to ask, "What on earth could this have been
for?"

As these children did already. You would see them squatting down over a pile of greeting cards, a pink nylon fluted lampshade, a polystyrene garden dwarf, a book, or a record, turning them over and over: *What was this for? What did they do with it?*

But these visits, these gifts, did not mean that in another mood, on another occasion, they would not kill. And because of a whim, a fancy, an impulse.

Inconsequence . . .

Inconsequence again, as with the departure of little June. We sat there and brooded about it, talked about it, listening: far above our heads there was the neigh of a horse, and sheep baaing; birds whirled up past our windows on their way to the top of the building, where there were the pickings of a farmyard for the effort of hopping through a broken window, was a vegetable garden, and even some trees. Inconsequence, a new thing in human psychology. New? Well, if it had always been there, it had been well channelled, disciplined, socialised. Or we had become so used to the ways we saw it shown that we did not recognise it.

Once, not long ago, if a man or woman shook you by the hand, offered you gifts, you would have reason to expect that he, she, would not kill you at the next meeting because the idea had just that moment come into his head . . . this sounds, as usual, on the edge of farce. But farce depends on the normal, the usual, the standard. Without the *norm,* which is the source of farce, that particular form of laughter dries up.

I remembered June, when she first robbed my flat and I asked Emily, "But why me?" The reply was: *Because you are here; she knows you.* Even: *Because you are a friend.*

We could believe that the children from upstairs might come down one night and kill us because we were their friends. They knew us.

One night, very late, sitting around the fire as it burned low, we heard voices outside the door and outside the window. We did not move or look for weapons. The three of us exchanged looks—it cannot be said that they were amused, no: we did not have so much philosophy, but I do claim these glances were of the order of humour. That morning we had given food to some of those brats who were outside now. We had sat eating with them. *Are you warm enough? Have another piece of bread. Would you like some more soup?*

We could not protect ourselves against so many: thirty or more in all, whispering beyond the door, below the window. And Gerald? No, that we could not believe. He was asleep, or away on some expedition.

Hugo turned himself, placing himself between Emily, whom he would defend, and the door. He looked at me, suggesting I should put myself between her and the window: of course it was Emily who must be defended.

The scuffling and whispering went on. There were some blows on the door. More scuffles. Then a burst of sound—shouts, and feet rushing away. What had happened? We did not know. Perhaps Gerald had heard of what they were doing, and had come to stop them. Perhaps they had simply changed their minds.

And next day some of the children, with Gerald, came down to us and we spent a pleasant time together. . . . I can say it, I can write it. But I cannot convey the normality of it, the ordinariness of sitting there, chatting, sharing food, of looking into a childish face and thinking, Well, well, it might have been you who planned to stick a knife into me last night!

And so it all went on.

We did not leave. If someone had asked, "Do you mean to say that you two people are staying here, in danger, instead of leaving the city for the country, where things are safe or

safer, because of that animal, that ugly, bristly old beast there
—you are prepared to die yourselves of hunger or cold or of
being murdered simply because of that beast," then we would
have said, "Of course not, we are not so absurd; we put human
beings where they belong, higher than beasts, to be saved at
all costs. Animals must be sacrificed for humans; that is right
and proper and we will do it, too, just like everybody else."

But it was not a question of Hugo any longer.

The question was, where would we be going? To what?
There was silence from out there, the places so many people
had set off to reach. Silence and cold . . . No word ever came
back, no one turned up again on our pavements and reported,
"I've come back from the north, from the west, and I ran
into so-and-so, and he said . . ."

No, all we could see when we looked up and out were
the low packed clouds of that winter hurrying towards us: dark
cloud, dark cold cloud. For it snowed. The snow came down,
the snow was up to our windowsills. And of all those people
who had left, the multitudes, what had happened to them?
They might as well have walked off the edge of a flat world.
. . . On the radios, or occasionally from the loudspeaker of an
official car, which, seen from our windows, seemed like the
relic of a dead epoch, came news from the east: yes, it seemed
that there was life of a sort down there still. A few people
even farmed, grew crops, made lives. "Down there"—"out
there"—we did hear of these places; they were alive for us.
And where we were was alive; the old city, near-empty as it
was, held people, animals, and plants which grew and grew,
taking over streets, pavements, the ground floors of buildings,
forcing cracks in tarmac, racing up walls . . . life. When the
spring came, what a burst of green life there would be, and
the animals breeding and eating and flourishing.

But north and west, no. Nothing but cold and silence.

We did not want to leave. And with whom? Emily, myself, and our beast—should we go by ourselves? There were no tribes leaving, no tribes even forming, and when we looked from our windows there was no one there on the pavements. We were left in the cold dark of that interminable winter. Oh, it was so dark, it was such a low thick dark. All around us, the black tall towers stood up out of the snow that heaped around their bases, higher every day. No lights in those buildings now, nothing, and if a windowpane glinted in the long black nights, then it was from the moon, exposed momentarily between one hurrying cloud and another.

One afternoon, about an hour before the light went, Emily was by the window looking out, and she exclaimed, "Oh, no, no, *no!*" I joined her, and saw Gerald out on the deep clean snow, high under stark branches. He wore his brave coat, but it was open, as if he did not care about the dreadful cold; he had nothing on his head, and he was moving about as if he were quite alone in the city and no one could see him. He was revisiting the scenes—so very recent, after all—of his triumphs, when he was lord of the pavement, chieftain of the gathering tribes? He looked about him at the exquisite crisp snow, up at the sky where low clouds were bringing dark inwards from the west, at the black trees touched up with white; he stood for minutes at a time, quite passive, staring, in thought or in abstraction. And Emily watched, and I could feel the fever of her anxiety rising. By now the three of us were there, watching Gerald; and of course other people were at their windows watching, too. He had no weapons. His ungloved hands were in his pockets, or hung at his sides. He looked quite indifferent, had disarmed himself, and did not care.

Then a small object hurtled past him, like a speeding bird. He gave a rapid indifferent glance at the building and stayed where he was. There followed a small shower of stones: from the windows above us catapults were being trained on him—perhaps worse than catapults. A stone hit his shoulder; it might have hit his face, or even an eye. Now he deliberately turned and faced the building, and we saw he was presenting himself as a target. He let his hands fall loose at his sides, and he stood quietly there, not smiling, but unworried, unalarmed, waiting, his eyes steadily on something or somebody in windows probably a story up from us.

"Oh, *no,*" said Emily again; and in a moment she had pulled around her shoulders a shawl, like a peasant woman, and she was out of the flat and I saw her running across the street. Hugo's breath was coming in anxious little whines, and his nose was misting the windowpane. I put my hand on his neck and he quieted a little. Emily had slid her arm under Gerald's, and was talking to him, coaxing him off the pavement and across the road towards us. There was a fusillade of stones, bits of metal, offal, rubbish. Blood appeared on Gerald's temple, and a stone, landing in Emily's middle, caused her to stagger back. Gerald, brought to life by the danger to her, now sheltered her with his arm, and he was bringing her in to the building. Above I could hear the children shouting and calling out, and their chant: "I am the king of the castle. . . ." The stamping and chanting went on above us as Gerald and Emily arrived in the room where Hugo and I waited for them. Gerald was white and there was a deep gash on his forehead, which Emily bathed and fussed over. And he made her look to see if the stone had hurt her much: there was a bruise, no worse.

Emily made him sit by the fire, and sat by him and rubbed his hands between hers.

He was very low, depressed. "But they are just little kids," he said again, looking at Emily, at me, at Hugo. "That's all

they are." His face was all incredulity and pain: I don't know
what it was in Gerald that could not—could not even now—
bear what those children had become. I do know that it was
deep in him, fundamental; and to give them up was to aban-
don—so he felt—the best part of himself.

"Do you know something, Em? The little one, Denis, he's
four years old—yes, he is. Do you know him, do you know the
one I mean? He was down here with me a few days back—
the little one, with the cheeky face."

"Yes, I do remember, but, Gerald, you do have to accept—"

"*Four,*" he persisted, "four. That's all. I worked it out
from something he said. He was born the year the first lot of
travellers came through this area. Yet he goes out with the
others; he is as tough as the others. Did you know he was on
that job—you know, the one that night?"

"A murder?" I asked, since Emily did not say anything,
but went on rubbing his cold hands.

"Yes, well—but it was murder, I suppose. He was there.
When I came back that night, I lost my temper—I was as sick
as I could be. I said to them . . . And then one of them said
that Denis had done it; he was the first to let go with what
he'd got—a stone, I think. He was the first, and then after
him the others—four years old. And when I came back into the
flat, do you know, the dead man was there, and they were all
. . . And Denis was there, as large as life among them, taking
his part. It's not their fault—how can it be their fault? How can
you blame a kid of four?"

"No one is blaming them," said Emily softly. Her eyes
were bright, and her face was pale, and she was sitting by
Gerald as if standing guard, protecting him, as if she had
rescued him and now would not let go.

"No, but if no one saves them, either, then that's the same as blaming them, isn't it? Isn't it?" he appealed to me.

We waited all night. Of course we were expecting an attack, a visit, an embassy—something. Above us, in the great empty building there was no sound. And all that following day it snowed, and was dark and cold. We sat and waited, and nothing happened.

I knew that Emily was expecting Gerald to visit the top part of the building, to find out what went on. She was meaning to dissuade him. But he did not go; and all he said was, after some days, "Well, perhaps they've moved somewhere else."

"And the animals?" said Emily, fierce, thinking of those poor beasts up there.

He raised his head and looked at her, and gave that short laugh which means someone has made an end to something in thought: a decision, but it is a decision beset with irony, or with conflict. "If I go up there—well, I might be pulled back in again—and that's no good. And, as for the animals, they have to take their chance like everyone else—there are other people up there still."

And so we went on quietly, the four of us.

It all came to an end, but I can't say when it was, after Gerald joined us. We had been there, waiting for winter to end, and we knew it was a long time, but not as long as our weary senses told us: an interminable time, but still not longer than a winter. Then, one morning, a weak yellow stain lay on the wall, and there, brought to life, was the hidden pattern. My feeling that this was what we had been waiting for was so strong that I called to the others, who were still asleep: "Emily—Emily! Gerald and Emily, come quickly. Hugo, where are you?"

From her room padded that obdurate beast, Hugo, and
behind him came Gerald and Emily, bundled in their furs,
yawning, dishevelled, not surprised, but looking their enquiry.
Hugo was not surprised, not he: he stood, all alert and
vivified beside the wall, looking into it as if at last what he
wanted and needed and knew would happen was here, and he
was ready for it.

Emily took Gerald by the hand, and with Hugo walked
through the screen of the forest into . . . and now it is hard
to say exactly what happened. We were in that place which
might present us with anything—rooms furnished this way
or that and spanning the tastes and customs of millennia; walls
broken, falling, growing again; a house roof like a forest floor
sprouting grasses and birds' nests; rooms smashed, littered,
robbed; a bright green lawn under thunderous and glaring
clouds, and on the lawn a giant black egg of pockmarked iron
but polished and glossy, around which, and reflected in the
black shine, stood Emily, Hugo, Gerald, her officer father, her
large laughing gallant mother, and little Denis, the four-year-
old criminal, clinging to Gerald's hand, clutching it and looking up into his face, smiling. There they stood, looking at
this iron egg until, broken by the force of their being there, it
fell apart, and out of it came . . . a scene, perhaps, of people in
a quiet room bending to lay matching pieces of patterned
materials on a carpet that had no life in it until that moment
when vitality was fed into it by these exactly answering
patches: but no, I did not see that, or if I did, not clearly. . . .
That world, presenting itself in a thousand little flashes, a
jumble of little scenes, facets of another picture, all imperma-
nent, was folding up as we stepped into it, was parcelling itself
up, was vanishing, dwindling and going—all of it, trees and
streams, grasses and rooms and people. But the one person I

had been looking for all this time was there: there she was.

No, I am not able to say clearly what she was like. She was beautiful: it is a word that will do. I only saw her for a moment, in a time like the fading of a spark on dark air—a glimpse: she turned her face just once to me, and all I can say is . . . nothing at all.

Beside her, then, as she turned to walk on and away and ahead while the world folded itself up around her, was Emily, and beside Emily was Hugo, and lingering after them Gerald. Emily, yes, but quite beyond herself, transmuted, and in another key, and the yellow beast Hugo fitted her new self: a splendid animal, handsome, all kindly dignity and command, he walked beside her and her hand was on his neck. Both walked quickly behind that One who went ahead showing them the way out of this collapsed little world into another order of world altogether. Both, just for instant, turned their faces as they passed that other threshold. They smiled. . . . Seeing those faces, Gerald was drawn after them, but still he hesitated in a fearful conflict, looking back and around, while the brilliant fragments whirled around him. And then, at the very last moment, they came, his children came running, clinging to his hands and his clothes, and they all followed quickly on after the others as the last walls dissolved.

## A NOTE ON THE TYPE

*This book was set on the Linotype in Granjon, a type named in compliment to Robert Granjon, but neither a copy of a classic face nor an entirely original creation. George W. Jones based his designs for this type upon the type used by Claude Garamond (1510–61) in his beautiful French books, and Granjon more closely resembles Garamond's own type than does any of the various modern types that bear his name.*

*Robert Granjon began his career as type cutter in 1523. The boldest and most original designer of his time, he was one of the first to practise the trade of type founder apart from that of printer. Between 1557 and 1562 Granjon printed about twenty books in types designed by himself, following, after the fashion, the cursive handwriting of the time. These types, usually known as* caractères de civilité, *he himself called* lettres françaises, *as especially appropriate to his own country.*

*The book was composed, printed, and bound by The Book Press, Brattleboro, Vermont. Typography and binding design by The Etheredges*